# faiThGirLz!™

# grace notes

## DANDI DALEY MACKALL

zonder**kidz**

ZONDERVAN.COM/
AUTHOR**TRACKER**

The children's group of Zondervan

www.zonderkidz.com

*Grace Notes*
Copyright © 2006 by Dandi Daley Mackall
Illustrations © 2006 by The Zondervan Corporation

Requests for information should be addressed to:
Grand Rapids, Michigan 49530

**Library of Congress Cataloging-in-Publication Data**

Mackall, Dandi Daley.
Grace notes / by Dandi Daley Mackall.
        p. cm. – (Faithgirlz)
Summary: Fifteen-year-old Grace Doe keeps an online journal–a weblog–about her classmates rather than trying to connect with them, until her anonymity is threatened and she realizes that God does not want her to be isolated.
        ISBN-13: 978-0-310-71093-6 (softcover)
        ISBN-10: 0-310-71093-6
        [1. Weblogs–Fiction. 2. Interpersonal relations–Fiction. 3. High schools–Fiction. 4. Schools–Fiction. 5. Christian life–Fiction. 6. Stepfamilies–Fiction. 7. Family life–Ohio–Fiction. 8. Ohio–Fiction.] I. Title. II. Series.
        PZ7.M1905Gra 2006
        [Fic]–dc22
                                    2005023527

Zonderkidz is a trademark of Zondervan.
Editor: Robin Crouch
Art direction: Laura Maitner-Mason
Illustrator: Julie Speer
Cover design: Karen Phillips
Interior design: Pamela J.L. Eicher

Illustrations used in this book were created in Adobe Illustrator.
The body text for this book is set in Cochin Medium.

Printed in the United States of America

07 08 09 10 • 10 9 8 7 6 5 4

So we fix our eyes not on what is seen, but on what is unseen.
For what is seen is temporary, but what is unseen is eternal.

*2 Corinthians 4:18*

# 1

## THAT'S WHAT YOU THINK!

By Jane

AUGUST 28

SUBJECT: BP GIRL

*Ever notice how right before some people go off or blow or explode, their eyelids flicker? Their lips squeeze together. Then those tendons in the neck turn into rope strands? No? You never noticed that?*

*Well, neither did poor Bouncy Perky Girl. Right before history class, she took it upon her perky self to demonstrate a new cheer for us. Bones was behind his desk already. (You remember my history teacher, Bones, as in "Dry as . . .") So BP Girl (Bouncy Perky) was midair when the bell rang. She couldn't stop because she was just getting to the part about Typical High fight-fight-fighting. Bones pushed himself up from his desk and walked over to BP Girl. She flashed him a Typical High cheerleader smile and moved into the win-win-win part of the cheer.*

*I saw what was coming a mile off, or at least fifteen feet off, from my seat in the back. Bones' eyelids twitched. His lips got even thinner.*

*It was like watching a train streaking toward a puppy on the tracks. Bones's neck turned into rope strands, and still BP Girl cheered on. I imagined the toe of a cowboy boot aimed and ready to deliver a blow to the puppy.*

*Bones screamed at BP Girl and ordered her to take her seat. She was totally surprised. You could have scraped her off the blackboard. I actually felt sorry for Bouncy Perky Girl.*

Grace Doe sat back and studied the computer screen. The blog entry wasn't bad. She'd have time to edit it before uploading to her website. She could answer a couple of the emails and respond to comments, then post those too. But first, she wanted to write about Jazz.

## · · · · · · · · · · · · · · · · · · · · · ·
## THAT'S WHAT YOU THINK!
SUBJECT: JAZZ

*There's this girl at Typical High, smooth and deep as Jazz. Lithe, with wild, black hair. She's got a moody wit that's mostly wasted at our school. Yesterday at lunch, Steroid Boy was bragging about becoming a vegetarian. I could tell he was trying to impress Jazz. But she kept eating from a box of animal crackers. When Steroid Boy finally stopped talking, Jazz said, "I'd offer you one of my animal crackers, but I couldn't live with myself if I brought on a crisis of faith for you." It was classic! But Steroid Boy just nodded, like he was agreeing with her.*

*I've been observing Jazz since school started. She doodles in her notebook margins. Cool sketches — kids, teachers, or just designs. I think she's the real deal.*

Gracie had been blogging — keeping an open journal, or "web log," on the Internet — for almost two months. And still, the only person who knew the identity of "Jane" was Gracie's little stepsis, Michaela. The only reason Mick the Munch knew about the blog was that Gracie needed the computer munchkin to set up the website and keep it running.

The door to Gracie's bedroom slammed open. She lunged to shut off the computer. But it was just Mick, in jeans and a Cleveland Indians baseball shirt. Her dark brown ponytail stuck out through the hole in her Indians cap. "Gracie, hurry up! Luke's waiting. You're going to make us late for school."

Gracie's stepbrother, Luke, was a senior at Big Lake High — blog name, "Typical High" — where Gracie was a sophomore. Mick's middle school was right next door, and Luke, under protest, usually drove them both to school.

"Coming," Gracie muttered, logging off.

Mick came over to the desk. "Did you get your bill from the server, Gracie?"

Gracie felt the familiar tightening in her stomach. "I said I'd handle it, Mick."

She was two weeks late on the payment for her website. She could pay it on Saturday, when she got paid for bagging groceries at Big Lake Foods. Until then, she just couldn't think about it.

She got up, ran her fingers through her short blonde hair, slid her cell into her backpack, and slipped into her flip-flops. Khaki pants, army green T-shirt — all set. One of the benefits of being invisible at school was that nobody noticed your wardrobe.

Luke had the motor running in his ghetto Ford. "About time," he called, shoving the passenger door open for Gracie. It didn't work from the outside. Mick hopped into the back.

"My fault, Luke," Gracie admitted.

Luke shrugged, turned up the radio, and headed down the drive. "Well, next time, I'm leaving without you."

Gracie believed him. Luke could be a pain. He treated her like she was five instead of fifteen, especially when he was around his girlfriend. Next year he'd be off to Ohio State, and Gracie figured he wouldn't give her a single thought. She was just the stepsister. Gracie had refused to attend the wedding three years ago when her dad married Lisa, Luke and Mick's mom. She'd hated the idea of a "blended family." Like all you had to do was dump kids from different gene pools into a blender and come up with a smoothie.

Since her parents' divorce, Gracie had been getting along okay living with her dad and seeing her mom whenever she bounced into town. Then, just like that, she'd gone from being the only child of Barry and Victoria Doe (the youngest and the oldest child) to being the middle child of Barry and Lisa Doe.

She liked Lisa. Luke could drive her postal, but Mick was impossible not to like. Still, Gracie couldn't shake the feeling that she was "odd man out" in the Doe household, which now included one-year-old twins.

Luke found a spot in the A parking lot, right between Mick's middle school and Big Lake High. A couple of senior girls pulled up next to them. He checked his hair in the rearview, even though it was too short to get messed up. Gracie had to admit that Luke Jenkins was good-looking.

Mick dipped out fast. "Thanks for the ride, Luke! I'm going to Ty's after school. Bye, Gracie!" Then she ran to catch up with Ty Fletcher, her baseball buddy.

Luke opened his door and called out to the girls who had climbed out of the car next to his: "Wait up!"

They stopped, smiled back at him, and waited.

"What about Jessica?" Gracie asked. But she'd been rooting for more than a month for Luke to dump his girlfriend. She was too fake for Luke.

Luke got out of the car. "Hey, I'm not married. Or dead." Then he walked off between the blondes.

Gracie trudged into Big Lake High alone, imagining that she was as invisible as the humid air that pressed in on her from all sides.

Inside, the halls buzzed. A senior couple leaned against the locker next to Gracie's. Behind her, two girls were arguing. A group of guys blocking the hall erupted in an explosion of laughter.

Gracie took out her recording notebook, leaned against her locker, and observed. This was where she got material for her blog. Three lockers down, Steroid Boy, whose real name was Bryce, was trying out his vegetarian routine on an unsuspecting freshman.

"Goes against my consciousness to eat meat," he told her.

Gracie jotted in her notebook: "Pupils dilated. He blinks four times. He touches his forehead twice. Steroid Boy is lying."

She couldn't even remember when or where she'd learned behavior signs like these. She'd read dozens of books about human behavior. But most of her real insights came from simply watching people. And taking notes.

Someone bumped her arm and kept walking. It didn't surprise her. Who says "Excuse me" to an invisible woman? Grace Doe had always been the kind of person nobody noticed or remembered. She'd come to accept that role and learned to take advantage of it.

Gracie looked up to see Annie Lind — blog name, Bouncy Perky Girl. Even without her brown and blue cheerleading uniform, Annie looked like a cheerleader — tall and bouncy, auburn hair, and giant blue eyes. She was surrounded by four hotties competing for her attention.

"True dat!" Annie cried, arm-punching Jared, Big Lake's star quarterback. "The boy's got game."

To be honest, Gracie had to admit Annie had never said a mean word to her. Then again, Gracie and Annie had hardly said any words to each other their whole freshman year.

Gracie waited until the bell rang to go to her first-hour class. Most kids took art their freshman year, which was probably why Gracie had waited until now to enroll as a sophomore. No one would ever accuse Grace Doe of following the crowd.

She floated to the back of the room, keeping her notebook handy. Gracie planned to be a writer, not an artist. Forcing herself to keep an online journal had been the best thing she'd ever done for her writing career. Her art, on the other hand, would never progress past the stick-figure stage, no matter how much she drew.

The art teacher, Ms. Biederman, couldn't have looked less like an artist if she'd tried. Kempt. That's the word Gracie had used in her notebook. The woman was entirely too neat and clean for art.

"Class, please?" Ms. B's voice grated on Gracie's nerves. "Today, paint something in this room. Make it representational. I want to be able to tell what you've drawn."

Chairs screeched as kids moved to the art cupboard. Most of them took the smallest poster board they could find, then pulled chairs around Ms. B's desk, where she'd set up a flower arrangement.

Gracie waited until the room settled. Then she sat down in front of the wastebasket, her back to the room, and tried to draw the rippled army green waste can.

Ms. Biederman spent most of the class time shutting people up instead of instructing them in how to draw. "People, please!" she whined. "Your mouths should not be moving!"

It took Gracie only fifteen minutes to draw the wastebasket, which ended up looking a lot like a barrel. She stood up and glanced around the room until she spotted Jazz, also known as Jasmine Fletcher. Nobody called her Jazz except Gracie, on the blog. Jasmine stood behind an easel in the back of the room. Her poster board looked three times the size of everyone else's.

Jazz didn't seem to notice as Gracie eased behind her. On the white board, red, blue, and yellow lines intersected, rose and fell. Gracie had never liked abstract art. She didn't "get" most of it. But this was different. Jazz had turned the poster board into something else. Gracie couldn't look away.

"Jasmine? What are you *doing*?" Ms. Biederman's voice sliced through Gracie's thoughts. She'd been so into Jazz's painting that she hadn't seen the art teacher creep up.

"What do you mean?" Jazz asked, her voice calm and controlled. But Gracie saw her jaw tighten, as if she were biting nails. Her body leaned away from their art teacher. Gracie recognized signs of anger when she saw them.

"What do I mean?" Ms. B's voice tripled in volume.

The flower-drawing crowd stopped smarting off and turned around.

"I *mean* ...," Ms. B continued, taking a deep, counting-to-ten breath, "draw something we can recognize, Jasmine. You still have time if you get going on it." She forced a smile at Jasmine, then rushed off to praise someone's daisy.

Gracie studied Jazz's picture again. She thought it looked almost familiar, as if the picture had been hanging in Gracie's locker for years. "What is it?" Gracie wasn't even sure she'd asked the question out loud.

But Jasmine must have heard. Without turning around, she answered, "A voice."

Gracie examined the way the red line got thinner as it peaked. The blue and yellow crossed low and thickened where they intersected. "It's Biederman's voice," Gracie muttered. Not an answer. Not a question. It was just there. Jazz had captured their art teacher's voice exactly.

Jasmine Fletcher turned around and narrowed her brown eyes at Gracie, as if she had just materialized. "Yeah," she said.

Gracie thought about telling Jasmine that her painting was amazing, that she'd captured the voice so clearly Gracie felt she could almost hear it — the rise, the sharp whine, then the disappointed growl. The painting spoke. It spoke to *her*.

But she didn't say anything.

Gracie watched silently as Jazz turned back to her easel. She lifted the poster board and ripped it down the middle. Then she joined the crowd around Ms. B's desk and painted flowers like the rest of them.

Gracie was still thinking about Jazz's painting when she got home from school. She needed to write about it, to blog it, so she could make sense of what had happened. She turned on her computer and went automatically to her in-box.

One email was marked with the red "!" for URGENT. The message was short and all in caps:

FINAL NOTICE! JANE'S BLOG WILL BE DISCONNECTED IF PAYMENT NOT RECEIVED BY 8–31.

Gracie stared at the notice. She couldn't lose her website. It was the only place she really belonged. She was finding her voice. She knew she wasn't there yet, not by a long shot. But she had readers, people who heard her. She had to keep blogging.

*If I lose that*, Gracie thought, the pain in her stomach coming back, *I really will be invisible.*

# 2

## THAT'S WHAT YOU THINK!

By Jane

AUGUST 29

SUBJECT: YOUR COMMENTS

*Dear Jane,*

*Your blog is all that! I've been trying to read my 'rents'
body language, especially my dad's. Like you're always
doing with people. I want to catch him chizzlin' — you
know, in a rare good mood, so I can hit him up for the car
keys. You keep writing about watching facial features, but
my dad ALWAYS has his nose in the newspaper. What can
I do?*

*—Fastcar*

*Hey, Fastcar,*

*Check out your dad's hands! Hands are the most*

*expressive parts of our bodies. You can see more in hands than in a face. Your dad's fingers will show you his emotions. Our fingers are so locked into our nervous systems that they're usually moving, even when we're reading. If his hands jerk, or if he turns the page suddenly, that's not a good time to ask. Wait until his shoulders aren't square and his hands relax. If he unbuttons his coat or loosens his tie while he's reading, or if he opens that palm, go for it!*

*— Jane*

*Dear Jane,*

*Nick and I have just been talking, but we're getting pretty tight. Still, I want to know if he's frontin' me. You know, faking how much he likes me? How can I tell if he's lying when he says I'm the one?*

*— Falling Fast*

*FF,*

*That's a pretty big question. Let me give you three basic gestures to look for. When someone's lying, check for: see no evil, speak no evil, and hear no evil. "See no evil" is when he rubs his eyes, or just touches one eye while he tells you something. He might wrinkle his nose too. The "speak no evil" gesture is when he touches his mouth while he's talking or uses his hands to block his words in some way. Look for a slight curling down at the corners of his mouth. "Hear no evil" is when he covers his ears or sticks his finger in his ear while he's telling you how great you are. The guy can lie, but his body language can't!*

—Jane

Gracie felt pretty confident answering most of the emails that people posted on her site. It was funny how easily she could "talk" to people on her blog. Not so in "real" life. Most of her blog readers wanted to know more about gestures and body language so they could read people the way she did. She could help them with that, and she wanted to.

But there were some questions she stayed away from, the ones asking advice about guy-girl relationships. She left all *love* emails as unanswered comments, although twice she'd had to tell readers that she didn't know anything about love or dating and couldn't help them. She'd hated having to write that. It was almost enough to make her wish she could get someone else to answer the "love" questions — someone like Annie Lind. Bouncy Perky Girl would have an answer for them.

Gracie hadn't gotten much sleep the night before. She was worried about the warning from her web host, worried about the money she owed her server. She'd written them again before she'd gone to bed, promising they'd have their money by Monday.

But that wasn't the only thing bothering her. Every time Gracie had bolted awake during the night, she'd been dreaming about Jasmine Fletcher. Gracie couldn't stop thinking about Jazz and her painting, about the scene she'd silently witnessed.

Maybe if she blogged about it, she could put the whole thing out of her head.

## • • • • • • • • • • • • • • • • • • • •
# THAT'S WHAT YOU THINK!
By Jane
SUBJECT: JAZZ

*Yesterday I witnessed the destruction of a masterpiece — and maybe of something more. Jazz, the doodler, tore up the coolest painting anyone had ever done at Typical High — all because our art teacher didn't get it.*

*I watched it happen. And I didn't say a word.*

*I think I could have stopped it. But I didn't say anything.*

*Do you ever feel like you know what you should say? Like you can almost hear this voice in your head telling you what you need to say to make things better? But you don't? I heard exactly what I should have said to Jazz: "Wow! That's sweet! It's the best thing anyone has ever done here. Don't change it. Can't you see how talented you are? You're a pro, Jazz!"*

*That's what I heard in my head and didn't say.*

*Where did it come from? The words I heard in my head? Sometimes I think that stuff could be coming from God.*

*No, I haven't knicked out or anything. I don't hear real voices in my head. It's just . . . sometimes I wonder.*

*I don't think I've blogged about God in the two months I've been writing here. It's not something I talk about — not that I do a lot of talking to people about anything. Sometimes I think that God and I would be just fine, if people didn't get in the way.*

*But they do. And when they get in the way, all I seem to do is step around them. Maybe I have enough faith to know what I ought to be saying or doing to help other people . . . just not enough faith, or courage, to do it.*

Luke drove to school again on Friday. He and Mick chatted away in the front while Gracie stared out the back window. The sun was up but stuck behind a bank of clouds.

"You guys need a ride after school?" Luke asked. "'Cause Jessica wants me to take her to the mall."

"Figures," Gracie muttered. Jessica and her friends might as well have packed their suitcases and moved into the mall permanently. Gracie didn't get it. She hated shopping, and so did Luke.

"I'm good," Mick answered. "Thanks, though. Ty and I are practicing after school." Ty Fletcher, who happened to be Jazz's brother, had been best friends with Mick since elementary school. They played baseball or catch nearly every day. Mick lived baseball. When Ty couldn't play, she practiced anyway, throwing the ball against the garage for hours.

Gracie could have used the lift home. She was working the evening shift at Big Lake Foods, and she had hoped to get some writing in first. But her shift didn't start until five, and it took her only twenty minutes to walk home. Luke probably would have dropped her off, but she didn't want him to resent her more than he already did. "I'm good too."

"Cool," Luke said.

Mick spent the rest of the ride pumping Luke for base-running strategy. Luke had played ball in middle school, then lost interest when he'd discovered girls. But Mick said he was great when he did play. Gracie was just glad Mick's mind was on her game. She hadn't brought up the website bill since yesterday morning. Gracie figured that with four hours of bagging tonight, she'd have enough cash to write a check that wouldn't bounce. The web host wouldn't get it until Monday, at the earliest. But hopefully, that would be soon enough. It had to be.

Notebook in hand, Gracie strolled the halls before class. With the weekend already here, the pressure was on for blog material. She jotted notes, but nothing stuck out.

She waited until the last minute to go to art because she really wasn't looking forward to seeing Jazz. But one glance around the room told her Jasmine Fletcher wasn't there. Everybody who was there was clustered at the end of the first row. Gracie couldn't see what or who they were gathered around. Then she heard.

"I still can't figure out why you call it Big Lake, Ohio," *snap* "when there's no lake. What is that about?" *Snap.* "Niagara Falls has a falls. Bear Mountain has a mountain. Hello?" *Snap.*

It was a voice Gracie hadn't heard. Phrases were punctuated by gum snapping. She tried to imagine how Jazz might paint this voice. Not whiney, like Ms. B's, but bold,

confident. A *look-at-me* voice. It reminded Gracie of her real
mom's TV voice, when she was being interviewed on child-
raising trends or the psychology of adolescence.

Gracie moved in close enough to get a glimpse of who was
talking. The girl had to be a good three inches shorter than
Gracie, who was five feet five. But this girl might as well have
been a giant, the way she commanded everyone's attention.
She was head-turning beautiful, with straight black hair to
her waist. She looked Polynesian. But she sure wasn't dressed
that way. A leather vest covered a pink T-shirt. She wore
sparkly tights under a lime green pouffy skirt. Her lime green
jellies matched her green hoop earrings. And she wore black
gloves with no fingers.

Gracie kept her distance and started taking notes. The girl
called herself "Storm. Storm Novelo." Kids stumbled all over
themselves asking her questions. Where was she from? How
did she like it here? Did she like art?

Storm laughed at that one. "Do I like art? Not as much fun
as hitting my head with a hammer, but close."

"Now, Storm," Ms. Biederman said, joking as if she'd
known the kid her whole life, "keep an open mind."

"Brains can fall out of open minds," Storm replied.

Ms. B didn't know how to handle that one.

Gracie took her seat. She wondered if "Storm" was a real
name. It didn't matter. The name fit.

Gracie didn't see the new girl again until lunch. No surprise
that she was at the cheerleaders' table. To hear better, Gracie
left her usual spot at the back and ventured closer, taking the
end of an almost-empty table.

"You'll really like Big Lake," Annie Lind promised in her bouncy, perky voice. She took a bite of her red Jell-O. "It's so fun!" Annie said everything like it was on a greeting card. Gracie wondered what it would be like to feel that happy all the time. "You should come by my mom's sandwich shop after school, Sam's Sammich Shop. We could get ice cream!"

"Ice cream is full of grooviness," Storm agreed. "Just promise me one thing — no Jell-O."

Annie stared at the raised spoonful of red Jell-O en route to her open mouth. "Okay." She sounded kind of hurt. "But how come?"

Storm sighed. "Do you know what's *in* gelatin? Boiled animal hooves, bones, and hides. Purified glue."

Gracie couldn't help laughing.

"How do you know so much about it?" asked Becca, a senior cheerleader.

Storm let out a girlish giggle at the exact moment she popped her gum. "I ... I heard it on TV. MTV, I think."

Gracie kept eavesdropping and recording notes. They really didn't need another wing-nut airhead at Big Lake High. But she had to admit that Storm was going to make good blog copy.

As she left the cafeteria alone, Gracie decided there were two kinds of kids in high school — the kids who were known by more people than she'd ever know, and the kids who knew more people than would ever know her. Clearly, Storm, like Annie, was in the first group. It was as obvious as the fact that Grace Doe was in the last.

After school, Gracie got home as fast as she could and changed clothes before starting her shift at Big Lake Foods.

She still had more than an hour to kill — time enough to check her site and see if any new questions or comments had been posted. She might even get a good jump on her first blog about Storm Novelo. Storm's blog name would be "New Girl." The column should just about write itself.

Gracie logged on. There were two questions from readers. Some guy wanted to know "Jane's" theory on lie detectors. Gracie took two minutes to explain that all lie detectors do is measure signs of nervousness, something the reader could do without a machine. He just needed to pay attention to the little signals people give without knowing it.

The second question was tougher:

> Dear Jane,
>
> My boyfriend is driving me crazy! When he's with me, he acts like I'm the only person in the world. But at school, he flirts with every decent-looking female in a 30-mile radius. What should I do?
>
> — Confused in Connecticut

Gracie had no idea how to answer that one. She felt bad for "Confused," but that was about all she could do. Maybe she should have Mick post a warning sign on the homepage: *No Love Answers Here*.

On the other hand, since Gracie was an expert in human behavior, she understood the way most of her species (i.e., teenagers) reacted to the word *no*. If she posted a message banning love questions, Gracie figured she'd probably get ten times as many of them. But sooner or later, she was going to have to do something.

All afternoon Gracie had been composing her next live journal entry in her head. It turned out that even though Storm was only a freshman, she was in three of Gracie's classes. So Gracie had lots of time to observe "New Girl."

• • • • • • • • • • • • • • • • • • • •

## THAT'S WHAT YOU THINK!
By Jane
AUGUST 29
SUBJECT: NEW GIRL

*A hurricane hit Typical High School today. Her name is "New Girl." She wears more makeup than the entire freshman class. It took her about two minutes to get what she wanted: the attention of everyone around her. If she hadn't grabbed my attention with her eight-point-on-the Richter-scale laugh, she would have had me with the gum chewing. Why do people think it's okay to chew gum with their mouths open, when they know it's not okay with other food? And don't they realize they're not the only ones in the room who have to listen to that little crackle pop they make with every chew?*

*It didn't take New Girl long to put down our fair city/town after only one day at school.*

*"You gotta love the suburbs," she announced in our last-hour history class. "They cut down trees and name streets after them."*

*When our history teacher lectured us about dysfunctional families and the decline of America, New Girl spouted, "Let's put the FUN back in dys-fun-ctional!" Then she rattled off all these state laws that are still on the books in our state. Did you know it's against the law here for women to wear patent-leather shoes in public? And on Sunday, it's illegal to fish for whales. (No, we're not in a whaling area.) But it's also illegal to arrest anyone on Sunday!*

Gracie felt she was on a roll and could have kept going for hours. But a new email popped up. She couldn't resist looking at it. As she skimmed the message, the ache in her stomach came back, double strength. She read the words again, letting each one sink into her, as if they were arrows.

> *Dear "Jane,"*
>
> *You are not Jane. "Typical High" is not Typical High. And guess what. I know. I know the real name of your high school. I know where it is. And very soon, I'll know exactly who you are. You're not anonymous anymore. I am on to you.*
>
> *CYAL8R — The Blog Buster*

# 3

Gracie read the threatening message again. That's how she looked at it. A threat. Somebody had figured everything out. She should have been more careful. How stupid was it to use the name "Jane"? At the time, she'd thought she was so clever. Jane Doe. Gracie Doe. She never dreamed anybody would make the connection though. After all, she was invisible in real life. How could she be "visible" in cyberspace?

Outside her window, Gracie heard the familiar *smack, smack* of the baseball slamming into Mick's mitt.

*Mick!* Gracie shoved back her chair and bolted for her open window. Below, Mick and Ty were throwing the softball hard, back and forth.

"Mick!" she screamed out the window. "Quick! I need you to come right now!"

"I'm working on my curve, Gracie," Mick shouted up. She threw again. The ball smacked into Ty's glove. "Can we do it later?"

"No! I need you now! Please!"

Mick shrugged. "Okay. We'll be right up."

"Alone! Sorry, Ty. Girl stuff." She liked Ty. But she couldn't let him in on this.

"I'm cool," Ty answered, tossing the ball into the air, then catching it himself.

Mick thundered up the steps and into Gracie's room. Her Indians cap was crooked, and dark, damp strands of hair hung across her forehead. "What's up?"

"You have to see this." Gracie sat back down in her desk chair and moved the mouse to get her screen back. "Read it, Mick. Somebody's found out about my website."

"You're kidding!"

Gracie tried to be patient as Mick frowned at the screen. "Well? What are we going to do, Mick? You're the tech genius around here. How could you let this happen?"

"Me?"

"How else could somebody find out I'm Jane? They must have traced it somehow." Gracie paced her room, actually paced. She'd read about people pacing. She'd even written stories where characters paced. But as far as she could remember, she'd never done it herself until now.

"I was careful," Mick said, chewing on her cheek, the way she did when Dad got on her case about playing ball too much and studying too little. "We've got a firewall. I can't imagine anybody tracking the site back to you."

Gracie stopped pacing. "I know it's not your fault, Mick."

Gracie made herself reread the message. "I just can't stand having anybody else know about the blog."

"When you think about it though, Gracie, why does it matter?" Mick's voice was soft, almost pleading. "Really. So what if somebody knows — ?"

Gracie spun around to face her stepsister. Mick didn't understand. "Nobody can know! Please, Mick. Nobody can figure out that I'm Jane."

"But I've been thinking, Gracie. You *should* take credit for the site. It's so tight! Your writing's great. You — "

"No!" Gracie felt panicked, as scared as if an actual stalker were breathing down her neck. "It would ruin everything if people found out!"

"Why?" Mick's voice, as always, stayed as calm as if she were the perfect parent instead of the little sister. Usually it worked. Mick's peace was something you could catch. It rubbed off on you.

Only not this time. "Because, Mick. Just because. Okay?" In her head, Gracie could have finished that explanation in a dozen ways: *Because Jane speaks up and says what she thinks, and Gracie could never do that ... Because people like Jane, and they don't like Gracie ... Because this blog is the only good thing in my life right now.*

"You *have* to get rid of this guy!" Gracie begged.

"Or girl." Mick stared at the screen. "Well, we don't need to post the comment."

"But he'll — or she'll — still be out there!" Gracie insisted.

"Listen, Gracie. It's probably just a hoax. Somebody thinking it would be funny to scare Jane. Do you know how easy it would be to write to every blog and say the same thing? I'll bet there are people out there with nothing better to do."

Gracie hadn't thought of that. A hoax. *Please, let it be a hoax.*

Mick went on. "Like a crank call. You know, where girls pick a phone number and call somebody and say, 'I know what you did. I'm on to you.' Wasn't that in some dumb movie? Maybe somebody saw the movie and translated it into cyberspace."

It made sense. It probably made more sense than anybody taking the time to figure out who was writing this blog. Out of all the thousands of live journal sites out there, why would any-body care about hers? "Do you really think it's a joke, Mick?"

"I do." Mick said it like it was fact. "So, can I go back to working on my curveball with Ty now?" Gracie studied Mick's face to see if she was as confident as she sounded. She wanted to believe the little munchkin.

"This really got to you, didn't it?" Mick asked, narrowing her brown eyes until they seemed to stare right through Gracie. "Okay, God," she said, not closing her eyes like a normal person talking to God. "Gracie needs you to give her a hug and let her know this is no big deal and you're still in charge. Help her see you in what she's doing. Help us depend on you more and listen to you. And if you want Gracie to stop being so secretive with the blog, you're going to have to show her, okay? Oh, and I pray for Blog Buster too, because it sounds like he — or she — needs to know you. You're so amazing, God! Thanks for caring about everything we're going through. Oh, yeah, and will you help me with my curve, please? Thanks again. Aren't you going to be late to work?"

Mick's prayers were so natural, so genuine, that it always felt like God was in the room. It took Gracie a second to realize the last question was addressed to her and the prayer was over. She had fifteen minutes to get to the grocery store.

Big Lake Foods was pretty good sized for a town of thirty thousand. But Big Lake, Ohio, was a university town, and university students ate big. As Gracie ran through the automatic doors, she stuck her observer's pad and pencil into the pocket of her khakis. Then she slid into her bagger's position at checkout three.

"Finally," Stan muttered. He was half a dozen years older than Gracie and worked her spot first shift. He'd only been there three weeks. Gracie doubted he'd last three more. Every inch of his body seemed coiled and ready to dash out the second Gracie arrived, which was usually fifteen minutes before the end of his shift.

"I'm still a minute early," Gracie informed him.

But Stan was already halfway to the exit.

"Hey, honey," Eileen called, waving a package of hamburger over the electronic counter until the numbers popped up on the register screen. Eileen had been head cashier at Big Lake for sixteen years. Gracie had already blogged about Eileen once. She'd made the point that if people are honest in their appearance, they can get away with almost anything. Eileen, for example, was a stout, down-to-earth woman who considered herself highly successful in her field, supermarkets. On anybody else, the orange red hair piled into a beehive, and held in place with enough bobby pins to set off airport security, would have been laughable. Same went for the thin pencil lines Eileen drew where her eyebrows should have been. But on Eileen Himmelberg, it all worked. She was Queen of the Supermarket in Gracie's book ... and on Gracie's blog.

Gracie had never talked that much with Eileen, but she'd always felt like she could have. "Sorry I'm *almost* late," she said, reattaching her "Hi! I'm Grace!" pin to her shirt.

"Sugar," Eileen said, standing over the computer, waiting to grab the long grocery receipt for the customer, "you okay?"

"Sure." She was and she wasn't. As hard as she tried to believe what Mick had said about crank emails, Gracie hadn't quite managed to get "Blog Buster" out of her head.

She turned to the elderly man in line, someone she'd seen come through a few times before. "Paper or plastic?" She was supposed to ask every customer every time, even though she knew his answer.

"Paper."

Gracie piled can after can of cat food into the paper grocery bag. This time he'd added flea spray to his usual purchases. Not a good sign. In fact, nothing he bought was a good sign — frozen fish sticks, Cheetos, two six-packs of beer, a chalky antacid, a pack of candy bars, and chocolate ice cream. She felt like she should say something to him. Cheer him up. Encourage him to eat broccoli, which happened to be on sale this week. Say something funny, something that would give him a bright spot in his dreary day.

Instead, she watched him shuffle away, leaning on his cart full of groceries as if it were the only thing holding him up.

Mick would have known what to say. She probably would've walked him to the car, both of them talking to each other and to God, their eyes wide open. He would have left with Mick's grin on his face.

Gracie was loading two cartons of eggs into a plastic bag when a familiar voice exploded behind her from checkout four. "Sweet! How did you get my name on a pin so fast? So this is my very own station? Fasheezy!"

Gracie peeked over her shoulder. Standing in the bagger's position one counter over, smacking her gum, was none other than "New Girl."

# 4

Gracie tried not to stare at Storm, but it was hard not to. She had a new look — orange flairs, a too-tight, too-short orange top, obviously designed to display the double gold hoops in her belly button. The girl's big smile flicked past Gracie without a sign of recognition.

"That must be the new bagger," Eileen said, handing Gracie a greeting card as she continued weighing then ringing up a woman's fruits and veggies.

Gracie stuck the card into a tiny brown bag and wondered how Storm could possibly have gotten hired at Big Lake Foods. "She's working here for real?" Gracie asked, wondering what Storm might have worn to the interview.

"Looks like it," Eileen answered. "Thank you, honey," she said to the woman, who waved off Gracie when she started to carry the bags for her.

Storm let out her showstopping laugh. "This is so fly!" she exclaimed. "Storm Novelo is officially a utility clerk!"

In her mind, Gracie pictured the gum-smacking Storm getting fired after two hours tops at Big Lake Foods. There was no way Eileen and the other cashiers would put up with her. Gracie wasn't the only one from her school who had a

job at BL Foods. Jeremy, a sophomore, worked in the back.
Wes did part-time stocking. Several of the kids worked on
weekends, although Gracie rarely saw them.

But this was different. Storm was already popular. And
Gracie didn't like the idea of one of the popular kids invading
her space. Didn't she get enough of that at school? It still
made her uncomfortable when Annie Lind or one of the other
cheerleaders came through her checkout. Usually, they just
bought pop or fashion magazines. Gracie always felt relieved
when they left.

Tammy Jo, the next cashier over, where Storm was
supposed to bag, was pretty tough. Gracie had worked with
her a few times and couldn't seem to do anything right. She
had a feeling there might be quite a bit of blogging material in
"The Tammy Jo and Storm Show." Gracie tuned out the other
voices around her so she could eavesdrop on them.

"You need to ask 'Paper or plastic?' for every customer,"
Tammy Jo instructed. She didn't sound too happy about
having to break in a new bagger. "Don't you go thinking for
the customer. You ask, hear?"

"Thanks, TJ!" Storm chirped.

Gracie had never heard anyone call Tammy Jo "TJ." It
didn't sound like a good idea.

"Seriously, I know nothing about this job," Storm admitted.
"I don't even *buy* groceries. I'm going to need everything you
can tell me. Let me know if I do something wrong. Promise?"

"Well, yes. I'll help you." Tammy Jo looked puzzled. But
Gracie was thinking that grouchy "TJ" had never sounded
so helpful.

"Paper or plastic?" Storm asked, as if the choices were gold and silver.

Gracie heard the woman answer, "Paper."

"Oooh," Storm said. "Are you sure? You want me to put the basket of apples in a paper sack?"

"Well," the woman stammered, "ye — yes. I guess. Why?"

"It's just that paper lets in oxygen, and plastic doesn't. And when the oxygen gets together with the ethylene gas that apples produce, well you've got yourself some fast-ripening apples. Not that I want to tell you what to do or anything. I mean, you'll be okay, as long as you take the apples right out of the bag when you get them home."

Gracie felt the urge to warn Storm. She knew Tammy Jo was going to yell at her to keep her mouth shut and do what the customer wanted.

But TJ didn't say a word.

"I never knew that," said the woman. "Plastic it is! Thanks … Stormy, is it?"

"Storm. And you're welcome."

Gracie, her back turned to Storm, heard the *thump, thump, thump* of apples being bagged.

"I personally love apples," Storm exclaimed. Everything she said was an exclamation. Gracie made a mental note that in her live journal, she'd record all of Storm's dialogue with exclamation points. "I don't eat apples," Storm continued. "Well, I do eat the peels from the yellow ones. But I love apple trees! Did you know they're related to rosebushes? If we didn't eat them, we'd all think they were gorgeous flowers! People call bananas the perfect fruit, because of the potassium, phosphorus, iron, calcium, vitamins A, B, C, and

$B_2$, I suppose. But to me, apples are the perfect fruit. There you go. Have a nice day!"

As usual, the later it got on Friday, the busier it got. People seemed to be meeting in the parking lot, huddling together, then descending to the checkout in waves. A whole hour went by when Gracie was too busy bagging to pay attention to what Storm was up to.

When the checkout cleared for a minute, it felt like the stillness between bad thunderstorms. Gracie turned around to see if Storm was still there. She was. An old woman, her checkbook open and ready, asked Tammy Jo, "Are these here grapes the kind without them seeds? I don't like grape seeds."

Tammy Jo held up the grapes. "Didn't you see when you picked these up?" It was somehow reassuring to have the real Tammy Jo back, the cranky one.

Storm took the grapes out of Tammy Jo's hands and dropped them onto the scale. "You can weigh them, TJ," she said. "They're seedless. Isn't it funny how we got seedless grapes? There was this one weird grape in Afghanistan. So somebody planted it by itself. And other seedless grapes grew. And there was another seedless grape in Iran. Same story. And every single seedless grape comes from those two — "

"You work here?" Callie, one of the freshman cheerleaders, hollered up at Storm. Sasha and Annie Lind were behind her, next in line. A guy was with them. Gracie was pretty sure he was on the varsity football team. Mick would have known. Gracie had seen him sitting next to Annie in assemblies and walking with her between classes. Nate. That was his name.

Storm stopped her spiel about grapes and looked as if she'd been caught stealing groceries instead of bagging them. "Hey!" she called, snapping her gum. "It's an ugly job, but somebody's got to do it. My 'rents swear it will build character. Like I need that! I consider my employment as community service, payback for all my high crimes and misdemeanors." She was talking and moving around like somebody had flipped her "On" switch.

The grape woman left, and the cheerleaders stepped up with their bottles of pop.

"I think this is a great job," Annie said, bouncy and perky as ever. "Plus, you get a paycheck. I help Mom at the shop, Sam's Sammich, and *I* don't get paid half the time."

"Man, that's not fair!" Nate said in a too-loud voice. "You should get paid. Minimum wage, at least!"

Callie, who was standing between Annie and Nate, gave him a raised-eyebrow glare.

Annie totally ignored him. "Anyway, Storm, can you come by the shop later? Or tomorrow maybe?"

"Maybe." Storm snapped her gum again.

Gracie tried to tune them out. She got enough of these people at school. It was weird though, the way Storm's voice changed. You never would have guessed this was the same person who'd been talking about grapes in the Middle East.

"Come on, Annie!" Nate pleaded, working his way next to her. She didn't even bother turning around. "You can't keep pretending I'm not here," he whined. "I made a mistake. Okay? I admit it."

"A mistake? Lying *and* cheating on Annie?" Callie demanded. "Or was the mistake the part where you got caught?"

"Hey, Storm," Annie said, still ignoring Nate, "do you know the difference between a man and a catfish?" Before Storm could come up with an answer, Annie answered herself. "One is a bottom-dwelling, scum-sucking leech. The other is a fish."

For once, Gracie was glad for Storm's obnoxious laugh. It covered her own. Again, she thought how easy it would be for Annie to answer the love emails that were piling up on the website. Gracie had heard Annie handle guys before, and it always surprised her. Wit didn't fit with her image of Bouncy Perky Girl. But it was there.

"Annie, come on," Nate begged. He opened his wallet and tried to pay for Annie's cola. The big spender.

Annie shut him down with one look.

"Annie," Nate whined, "let's go out tonight. We can talk. Okay?"

Annie smiled sweetly at him. "Sorry, Nate. I don't date outside my species."

Storm laughed so loud that everyone in that end of Big Lake Foods turned to stare at her. "You go, girl!" she shouted after Annie. "See you guys later!"

And she would — see them later. Gracie was sure of that. It amazed her how easy it had been for Storm to get into the popular group, when so many girls at school tried so hard to be part of that little clique. Storm had just shown up. And she was in.

Gracie glanced back in time to see Storm smiling and waving good-bye to her new friends. Her orange bracelets jangled, and the gold belly rings were on full display.

Then something amazing happened. Gracie saw Storm's mouth melt. The smile dropped, then seeped away. It was like watching a stoplight change from green to red, with no yellow in between. The laugh wrinkles above Storm's eyes and above her upper lip turned flat. Her shoulders sagged.

And then it was over. Storm turned to Tammy Jo, and the smile was back. She said something to her and let out that deep, snorting laugh.

But in that instant in between, when Storm Novelo must have believed that nobody was looking, Gracie had glimpsed another Storm. And she was pretty sure *that* Storm was the saddest person she'd ever seen.

# 5

For the last hour of her shift, Gracie observed "New Girl" every chance she got. She couldn't get Storm's pained, sad look out of her head. It made her think of Jazz's expression right before she tore up her painting.

Gracie couldn't keep ignoring these nudges she was getting. She wondered if maybe God let her notice these things because he wanted her to do something. But what could she do? She decided she'd at least say something to Storm. Maybe Storm would open up about whatever was making her so sad. Gracie couldn't imagine that she, Invisible Grace, would be able to say anything to help.

Gracie kept glancing back at Storm, waiting for a break in the flow of customers. Storm had all the cashiers laughing. A couple of them even begged Eileen to put Storm with them next time. Customers loved her too.

"You're buying a Frisbee?" Storm squealed to a guy in a Big Lake University sweatshirt. "I love Frisbees! What's not to love? That cute, little flying-saucer look they've got going for them! You know, last year more Frisbees were sold than baseballs, footballs, and basketballs combined. So what's with not having university Frisbee competition?"

The guys were into it, inviting Storm to meet them on the quad for an ultimate Frisbee game that night.

She never let up. She worked the crowds all evening. Storm seemed so totally fun-loving and happy that Gracie wondered if she'd imagined the sadness. But she was usually right-on in reading people.

Gracie finally got the courage to approach her just as the shift was ending. She walked to Storm's station, with no idea what she was going to say. "Hi," she managed to utter. She was so lame at conversations. Even in that one word, Gracie knew she sounded like a total loser.

"Gotta bounce!" Storm did a kind of pirouette, grinned and waved, then dashed away.

Gracie watched her leave. Maybe she'd been wrong about Storm. Time would tell. Monday at school Gracie planned to keep an eye on the Storm.

Gracie had to wait around to pick up her paycheck. Mr. Hawkins wrote it up for her as a favor instead of making her wait until Monday. As soon as she got home, she made out the check for her website. Then she wrote up the deposit slip so she could do the walk-through deposit first thing in the morning on her way to work. Just having things ready to mail helped ease the worry.

When Gracie got home, she was too wound up to sleep, so she finished off Friday's live journal entry and started the one she'd planned for Saturday:

• • • • • • • • • • • • • • • • • • • • • • •

# THAT'S WHAT YOU THINK!

By Jane

AUGUST 30

SUBJECT: PURPLE VANS AND BELLY BUTTONS

*New Girl had a new look today — flairs, very short top. She periodically displayed her belly-button jewelry. And I'd like to know why that's okay. Is it the whole "purple minivan" thing? When purple minivans first came out, didn't you just want to barf? Of course you did. I was just a little kid, but I knew enough to want to hurl when I saw one. After a while though, I stopped gagging. Now I barely notice them. (Don't get me wrong. If I'm ever behind the wheel of a purple van, you have my permission to crush both of us with the nearest eighteen-wheeler.)*

*The point is that we've gotten used to stuff — like words that used to shock, purple vans, and belly-button jewelry. Tell me there aren't at least a couple of better places to put your jewels.*

Gracie sat back and read what she'd written. Lately, everything she wrote seemed to be a big gripe. She didn't mean it that way. She was grateful she had a place where she could be funny or let off a little steam without hurting anyone. But she didn't want people to get tired of *That's What You Think!* or of "Jane." Maybe she needed a different approach for tomorrow's blog.

# THAT'S WHAT YOU THINK!

By Jane

AUGUST 31

SUBJECT: DID YOU KNOW...?

*Did you know that brown rice is better for you than white rice? Well, of course you did. Evidence: school cafeteria ladies serve white rice, along with other nourishing foods, like french fries, hot dogs, and grease-burgers. But did you know why brown rice is better? It's because brown rice doesn't have the outer layer of bran polished off. And did you know that "wild rice" is NOT really rice? It's brown seeds of a grass that grows mostly in swamps. But it's in Michigan, Minnesota, and Wisconsin too. Native Americans used to harvest the stuff in their canoes, which is why they were so healthy until the settlers introduced them to diseases.*

*And speaking of Native Americans, the Narragansett gave us squash. They called it "askatasquash," but the colonists couldn't pronounce it and just went with "squash."*

Gracie had found it all pretty fascinating, and so had everybody else at Big Lake Foods, when Storm had spouted off her food trivia. Gracie felt kind of guilty for taking Storm's material now. But the truth was that on her own, she'd probably never come up with enough fun, interesting food facts to fill a whole column on the blog.

She would have loved to do a funny column like this one now and then, something full of fascinating facts. It would break up her human-interest observations and keep readers off guard. But where would she get that kind of info? And even if she could come up with enough odd facts, when would she find time to write one more thing? She'd just started her sophomore year, and already she felt behind with homework. She was a day late with the rough draft of her English paper. And she had a history test next week covering three chapters she hadn't even read yet.

Gracie was pretty sure Storm wouldn't care about having her trivia facts appear without posting her name for credit. She had bigger and better things on her mind — like Annie and the cheerleaders, or those BLU guys and their Frisbee. Besides, Storm really didn't seem to like it when people noticed how much she knew about a subject. Still, as a journalist, Gracie decided she couldn't take credit for a column that wasn't all hers.

. . . . . . . . . . . . . . . . . . . .

## THAT'S WHAT YOU THINK!
By Jane
SUBJECT: TWO FACES OF NEW GIRL

*I'd like to take credit for the fascinating food facts above. But they came from New Girl. That's right — the very same New Girl who acts like she's missing brain cells when she's in a crowd. She's got facts like that — and a lot more — ready to give off the top of her head. I'm afraid I settled for surface observations when I wrote about her before. Today I saw through her. She's loaded with facts and even intelligence, I think. It's like another New Girl lives inside the ditzy one everybody sees. Today I watched her with her new friends, and she was the center of attention, laughing and cracking wise. You would have thought they'd been best buds forever. Not a care in the world.*

*Then I caught a look. In the second after the friends left and before she turned to another audience, New Girl's face collapsed into the saddest expression I've ever seen. I may be wrong, but I'm thinking that the empty-headed, giggling front she shows people is fake. Another New Girl, maybe the real New Girl, stays hidden inside.*

*What if inside every "dumb blonde," lived an intelligent woman crying to get out?*

*If I were a stronger person, maybe I could help her come out. I felt that urge again, like a "still, small voice," a nudge from God, to step up and talk to her. Believe it or not, I tried this time. I got out one word, "Hi."*

*I don't think she heard me. Or saw me. Guess I'm still invisible.*

# 6

Saturday morning when Gracie came down for breakfast, Dad had already gone into the office for an early meeting. He worked all the time, Gracie thought. Sometimes she went days without even seeing him.

Lisa was doing battle with the twins ... and losing. David and Daniel were throwing Cream of Wheat at each other, but most of it seemed to be landing on their mother. At eleven months, the boys still weren't talking — at least not to other humans. They talked to themselves though. Gracie was convinced they understood each other perfectly.

"Hey, guys!" she called, crossing to the fridge in search of blueberry yogurt.

"Eraugh!" David screamed in her general direction.

"Arurgh!" Daniel agreed.

Gracie gave up on the yogurt hunt and closed the fridge door. "Oh, yeah?" she said, crouching and creeping up on the boys, her hands raised in tickle position.

"Aaaaaah!" David cried, already laughing as if she'd tickled him within an inch of his life. Daniel followed suit, and it became a screeching contest.

"Doesn't anybody just say 'Good morning' anymore?" Lisa asked. But she was laughing too. Lisa Doe couldn't weigh more than a hundred pounds. She had to stand on tiptoes to hit five feet. Officially, she was Asian-American, but China was so far removed from her family's past that even her grandmother spoke perfect English, and only English. Gracie thought Luke was the only one of Lisa's kids who looked at all Asian, even though he was almost as tall as Gracie's dad. Luke had his mother's eyes and her thick, black hair.

When Lisa and Gracie's dad had returned from their honeymoon in Hawaii, they'd collected their "blended" kids and moved into the new house. Gracie hadn't known what to expect, especially since the last time she'd spoken to Lisa and Dad had been on their wedding day — a phone call to the church to inform them she wouldn't be coming.

"I'm not calling you 'Mom.'" That was the first thing Gracie had said to Lisa as Dad carried in the honeymoon bags and suitcases.

Lisa had walked over to the kitchen table and sat down with Gracie. With a perfectly straight face, she'd responded, "Good! And I'm not calling *you* 'Mom' either."

It hadn't taken long for Gracie to realize that she'd lucked out in the stepmom department. Sometimes she believed she might feel part of this family if she would just let herself. But something inside her made her keep her distance. Maybe she was afraid of betraying her real mom. Or maybe she just didn't know how to be a part of anything.

Mick appeared in the doorway. "Mom, aren't you ready yet?" *She* was ready — bat and glove in hand.

"Two minutes, Mick." Lisa glanced at the kitchen clock, a yellow daisy orb above the microwave. "Make that twenty minutes. And you'll still be early."

"You're not dressed," Mick informed her.

"What do you mean?" Lisa twirled in her pink-flowered nightgown. "I bought this especially for your games." She turned to Gracie. "Gracie, can you watch the boys while I drive Mick to her practice? Your dad could be back any minute."

"As long as one of you gets home by 9:40," Gracie answered. "I'm working today."

"Again?" Lisa and Mick said it in unison. Then Lisa went on solo. "Does your father know you're working so many hours?"

"I doubt it. How would he know when he's never around?"

Daniel banged his high chair, as if agreeing with her. Their dad traveled a lot. Lately though, he'd been in town. But he spent a lot of evenings and even weekends at the office. "Barry Doe, Advertising Executive." That's what the little silver nameplate on the door of his office said the one time he'd taken Gracie with him to work. Taking his daughter to the office hadn't been his idea.

Gracie remembered the whole day, even though she hadn't even started school yet. Victoria — which is what her mom had always insisted Gracie call her — had received a last-minute invitation to appear on TV, probably to comment on child development because that's what she wrote books about. They couldn't get a sitter, so Gracie had spent the day at Dad's office. Even though he worked in a different office building now, she still pictured him in the skinny gray building, behind the brown door with the silver nameplate on it.

"No, no, no, no, David," Lisa pleaded, wrestling his spoon out of his clenched fist. He'd joined Daniel in the high-chair-banging band, then taken the activity to new heights.

"Dad's home!" Mick cried, running to the window. She'd started calling Gracie's dad "Dad" even before he'd married Lisa. Luke still spent one or two weekends a month at their real dad's house in Cleveland. Not Mick. Even though Greg Jenkins lived forty minutes away from Big Lake, Mick saw him only on holidays, if that. She didn't seem to mind.

Gracie heard the car creeping up the driveway.

"Wonder if it's a good sign or a bad sign that the meeting's over already," Lisa mused, trying to wipe Daniel's mouth.

Mick shoved the window up and hollered out, "Dad! Can you come to my practice?"

Gracie couldn't tell if Mick got an answer. The car door slammed, and Dad came in through the back door. "Wow. The gang's all here. Morning, everybody."

It occurred to Gracie that if her dad's company ever needed to do a commercial on the average John Doe, they should star her dad, Barry Doe. He was six feet and in pretty good shape, except for the twenty pounds that had stuck to his stomach, thanks to Lisa's good cooking. With receding brown hair and unstylish glasses, he'd never been quite sophisticated enough for the first Mrs. Doe. Gracie wasn't even sure how she knew this, but she did.

Lisa took time out from fighting David for the washcloth to cross over and give her husband a kiss. Gracie had no memories of her real mom kissing her dad.

"Is it good or bad that you're home already?" Lisa asked, her arm still around his waist, although she had to stretch to keep it there.

"Good. Very good," he answered. "I gave a record-breaking twenty-nine-minute presentation. And they gave a record-breaking sixteen-minute thumbs-up. They're going with my idea for the midsize model."

"That's great!" Lisa exclaimed. "My hero! So, do we get a free car for a bonus?"

"I'll have to bring up that part of the campaign on Monday," Dad teased. He turned to Mick, who had been waiting patiently for her turn. "Mick, I can't make it to practice, honey. I've still got all the paperwork to do. And I've got to get it in the mail by noon. Sorry."

"That's okay. It's just practice." Mick glanced up at the clock. "And now we really do have two minutes, Mom. We promised to pick Ty up, remember?"

"I know. I'm almost ready!" Lisa raced off, calling back from the stairs, "Barry, you've got the kids until I get back!"

He sighed. As if only now spotting Gracie, he grinned at her. "What are *you* doing today?"

"Hanging out at the grocery store with all my buddies," Gracie said, moving toward the door.

"You're working again? Are you sure you have enough time to study? Your homework comes first."

This was not the first time she had heard that one. "I'm okay, Dad."

The twins began kicking their high chairs in almost perfect unison.

"What's Gracie okay about?" Luke yawned from the doorway. One side of his face was creased, as if he'd just pulled his face from the pillow, which, judging by his pajamas, he had. "Do I smell bacon?"

Dad sniffed the air. "I don't think so."

"Could I smell bacon? Please?" Luke had Gracie's dad wrapped around his little finger in a way Gracie had never managed to pull off.

"Okay. That's one thing I can cook." Dad rolled up the sleeves of his pale blue dress shirt. "Luke, set the twins free. Then keep an eye on them."

Gracie kissed the tops of the twins' heads as Luke set them down from their high chairs. "Later, guys. I've got to get going. Break a leg, Mick."

"It's not a play, Gracie. But thanks anyway."

Grace's morning shift at Big Lake Foods proved to be busy but uneventful. Apparently, Storm had better things to do than serve in her post as "utility clerk." True, that *was* the official name for a bagger. But Gracie had never heard it used by anybody except Storm. Maybe "New Girl" had had enough of the grocery-store life.

The rest of Saturday was weird. The cashiers did their business, but nobody joked around. Even Eileen seemed depressed, forgetting to say "thank you" to customers. Gracie knew they missed Storm. Her absence made it feel like somebody had died. How did Storm do that? Gracie wondered as she operated on automatic pilot — cans on the bottom of bags, bread on top. Storm Novelo was the center of attention . . . and she wasn't even there.

By the time Gracie got home after work, all she wanted to do was go to bed. Lisa had kept a plate of spaghetti warm for her, so she ate that first. Then she remembered all the homework she had to do.

In her room, she tried to write her English paper, an essay comparing any two short stories they'd read in class. She'd picked the two shortest ones. Now she wished she'd put more thought into it. Her two stories didn't seem to have much in common. She was working out her introduction when Victoria popped up on IM.

. . . . . . . . . . . . . . . . . . . . . . . . . . . . . . . . . . . . . . . . .

**Grace:**      **Victoria, is that you???**

Victoria:      Hi, sweetheart! How's my fave daughter? Wish
               you were here! August in Paris is almost as
               beautiful as April in Paris!

**Grace:**      **What are you doing in Paris?**

Victoria:      Didn't I tell you? They want me to do a TV talk
               show with that French boy who wants to divorce
               his parents. Hope my français is still okay.

**Grace:**      **I'm sure it's great. They'll love you!**

Victoria:      Speaking of "love," I met Somebody. (Don't tell
               your father!)

**Grace:**      **Is he nice?**

Victoria:      Gorgeous! And how about you? Any new
               boyfriends?

**Grace:**      **You know. Same o. Same o.**

Victoria:      Cell phone's ringing, honey. Have to run! Love
               you!!!!!!!!!!!!!!

**Grace:**      **You too, Victoria!!**

**Grace:**      **Victoria?**

**Grace:**      **You there??**

Gracie signed out. She hadn't heard from Victoria in two
weeks. There were so many things she should have asked her.
Told her.

But still, it had been good to hear from her at all. Gracie was glad they'd thought to put each other on their buddy lists. She could only imagine how many "buddies" her mother had on her list. How sad was it that the only "buddies" on *Gracie's* list were her stepsister, a grandmother who never used Instant Messaging, an aunt she'd met only once, and a mom named Victoria?

Gracie was about to shut down when the "New Mail" box appeared. For a second she hoped it was her mother again. Maybe Victoria had too much to say to put into an instant message.

As soon as she clicked on the icon, she saw that the message had routed through her website and was addressed to Jane.

> *Jane, why didn't you answer my last email? That wasn't very friendly of you. You're a good writer, and I'd like to meet you face-to-face. Who knows? That may happen sooner than you think. Maybe Monday we'll bump into each other in the halls of BL High — oops, I mean Typical High.*
>
> *L8R! — Blog Buster*

# 7

Gracie stared at the computer screen. *BL High?* Big Lake High! *Blog Buster* wasn't a hoax. He — or she — knew the name of Gracie's high school.

Gracie hit the Print icon, grabbed the copy from her printer, and ran to Mick's room. She knocked but couldn't wait for an invitation. "Mick!" she called, turning the knob and barging in. The room was dark, except for a streak of moonlight that split the tiny room in two.

Crossing to Mick's bed, Gracie whispered, "Mick? You awake?"

Mick jerked straight up in bed. "What? What happened?"

Gracie turned on the bedside lamp and sat on the bed. "Plenty. Read this." She handed Mick her glasses. The light spilled onto Mick's walls, which were covered with Cleveland Indians posters. A couple of the players didn't even play for the Tribe anymore, but Mick couldn't let them go. Her room was about half as big as Gracie's. Even Luke's basement room was smaller than Gracie's, a fact he pointed out at every opportunity. Gracie figured she'd been given the best room out of pity, but she took it anyway.

Mick set down the paper, put her glasses back on the nightstand, and rubbed her eyes. "I could have been wrong about this being a hoax."

"No kidding! Blog Buster is waiting to pounce on me at school Monday. What am I going to do, Mick?" It was crazy to dump this on her little sister. But she didn't have anybody else to talk to.

"Maybe you should talk to Mom and Dad," Mick suggested.

Mick had tried to get Gracie to involve their parents from day one, but Gracie thought of the blog as a diary. Diaries had keys for privacy, and kids didn't turn over their keys unless their parents made them, right? Lisa and Dad trusted Gracie and Mick on the Internet. Luke too. They'd set up clear rules, and Gracie followed them. The blog was something she wanted to do on her own. "Can we try to handle this first, Mick? If it gets creepy or anything, we'll call in the troops. Okay?"

"Promise?" Mick didn't look happy about it.

"Promise."

Mick sighed. "Okay. So, think. Who could Blog Buster be?"

"Has to be a student at Big Lake," Gracie reasoned. "He must have recognized the teachers and kids there and made the connection."

"Okay," Mick agreed. "That makes sense." She slipped on her glasses again and reread the message. "They don't say that they know *you* — just Big Lake High."

"That's true," Gracie conceded, trying to latch on to that speck of hope. Maybe Jane was still anonymous, even if Typical High wasn't.

"So," Mick continued, "if you just act normal — "

"Right. Ask the impossible."

"You know what I mean."

They were silent for a minute. Gracie was running through a list of possible Blog Busters. Science geeks? Math brains?

Had to be somebody smart, or at least somebody who could read. That eliminated cheerleaders and jocks.

"What will you do if someone walks right up to you and asks if you're Jane?" Mick asked. "You can't lie."

*Maybe I can*, Gracie thought. She didn't say it though.

Mick yawned and checked her alarm clock. "Gracie, it's too late to think straight. We have all day tomorrow to work out a plan for Monday."

"I guess," Gracie admitted. She knew she wouldn't get any sleep tonight, but that didn't mean Mick had to suffer. She got up and turned off Mick's light. "Thanks, Mick. 'Night."

Morning was a long time coming. For possibly the first time ABF, "After Blended Family," Gracie was the first one up on a Sunday morning. Lisa was an early riser, and the twins never slept in. On Sundays Lisa worked an hour to get the boys ready for church. Rounding up the rest of the family took almost as long. It was the only morning they all ate breakfast together — pancakes.

Gracie knew it wouldn't do any good to say she didn't feel like going to church. It might have worked when she'd lived alone with Dad. But Lisa was a different story. Now, unless you were dying *and* contagious, the Doe family went to church.

Outside the kitchen window, the gray morning blended skies with clouds as Gracie watched Lisa pass the syrup around the breakfast table. The twins fed each other with fistfuls of pancakes. Mick ate fast, stealing glances at Gracie.

Gracie picked at her pancakes, while Luke told them about his calculus teacher, who was a genius with numbers but not with words. The guy couldn't speak in complete sentences because numbers kept popping into his head or something. Gracie couldn't follow the conversation, but no one seemed to notice. Or care. At one point, her dad laughed so hard at something Luke said that he sprayed coffee. That set off the twins, and they started spitting apple juice all over the kitchen.

Gracie's youth group met first hour in the church basement. She took a back seat and tried to pay attention, but her mind wouldn't untangle from visions of Blog Buster cornering her.

The screech of chairs on the linoleum floor brought her to attention. Kids were standing up and pulling their seats into small circles.

"Earth to ... what's your name again?" asked a tall, lanky guy Gracie had seen in youth group off and on last year. "Don't tell me. Jill? No, Jan?"

"Grace," she answered. But she studied his face. Jill? Jan? If I'd let him keep guessing, would he have guessed "Jane"? What if he's the Blog Buster?

"Right," he said. "Grace. That's it. I'm Ryan."

She knew his name. He went to Hillside, not Big Lake. No way he could have written that email. She had to quit thinking about Blog Buster, or she'd go crazy.

They formed small groups, with six or seven in each. Everybody was supposed to report how school was going. They had to share their biggest worry about the rest of the school year. Gracie's group took turns, going around the circle. When they got to her, she said, "I'm worried about keeping up with all the homework." Then she turned to the guy next to her, and it was over.

If only homework were her biggest problem ...

For the main service, Gracie and Mick sat with Lisa and
Dad, while the twins slugged it out in the nursery. Luke
always sat in the back pew with his buddies. Gracie might
as well have stayed home. She couldn't have said what the
sermon was about. If there'd been a quiz, she would have
scored zero.

On the drive home, Dad swung by the DQ fast-food
window and let everybody order takeout. Lisa never ordered
anything exactly as it appeared on the menu. She leaned
across Dad to ask for extra lettuce, no onion; double cookie
dough in her Blizzard; and onion rings instead of fries, with
a special request to undercook the onion rings, please. Mick
wasn't much better. She changed her mind twice. And Luke
had to be convinced that three sandwiches would too make
him sick. Gracie didn't want to order anything because her
stomach felt like pea soup was bubbling in it. But she gave in
and got a milk shake, just so they could get out of there. By
the time the Does got their food, the line of cars behind them
wound behind the building.

"Great sermon, wasn't it?" Lisa asked when they were on
their way again.

Mick was sitting between Gracie and Luke in the way-
back, while the twins took up the middle seats. "I love that
whole part in Corinthians," Mick agreed. "You know, about
how we're *part* of a body. Not the whole body. I don't even
care if I'm an arm or a leg or a toenail. It's just a good feeling
to belong." Mick elbowed Gracie.

Gracie stared out the window. She had heard the Scripture
before — that each Christian is a part of a whole body.
Belonging to Jesus felt like a given. Where Gracie had trouble

was fitting into a body, belonging with other people. Grace Doe had never belonged with anything, never been a part of anything. Not really.

Mick was another story. She'd always been on teams. She joined school committees. Mick seemed to belong everywhere, especially in church. The Munch loved church. All of her friends, except Ty, went to their church. And she even brought Ty sometimes.

Mick was definitely a people person. Grace Doe was not, and never could be. Last year for her birthday, Luke had given her a T-shirt that read "Do I *look* like a people person to you?" At least she was good at observing the species. Gracie could still see Jazz in art class, the way her face had tightened into anger when Ms. B told her to start her painting over. Jazz hadn't reacted, not with words. But Gracie had watched as the anger dissolved into pain. Gracie was pretty sure she'd been the only one to see it.

And what about Storm Novelo? Everybody at Big Lake High accepted the fact that this new girl, although slightly ditzoid, was happy. But Gracie had seen what she was almost certain nobody else had — the instant of sadness that had flashed through Storm like an electrical current, a flash of lightning.

Gracie had seen, observed, as she did now, peering back through the drizzle-streaked rear window at other churches letting out. August was supposed to be hot and dry, but it had rained almost every day. People joked about the weather in Cleveland, where, according to Clevelanders, it had been partly cloudy since 1930. Maybe September would be better.

Sunday afternoon the rest of the family, plus Ty, watched the
Indians game on TV in the Doe living room. From her room
upstairs, Gracie could hear them cheer and boo — mostly
boo — while she read her history chapters and finished her
English essay. She tried not to think of the fact that Ty fit into
her family better than she did. She checked her buddy list to
see if Victoria might be online. She wasn't, and there were no
messages from her.

The lack of sleep caught up with Gracie, and it was all she
could do to wash her hair and fall into bed by nine o'clock.
She slept soundly for about two hours. Then she woke up and
couldn't get back to sleep. The rest of the night, she wrestled
with visions of Blog Buster waiting for her at Big Lake High.

Monday morning Gracie stared out the smudged window
as Luke drove to school. He tuned the radio to WROK and
cranked up the volume. Gracie's head pounded with every beat.

Mick leaned up from the backseat as soon as Luke pulled
into the parking lot. "Do you really think Blog Buster will be
there waiting for you?" she whispered. "Want me to walk in
with you?"

Gracie would have loved to have Mick stay with her all day.
But that would only delay disaster. She shook her head. "I'll
be okay. Thanks, Mick."

She could feel Mick watching her as she walked through
the lot and on into Big Lake High. Gracie tried to look
as normal as possible. She was wearing black jeans and a
wordless black T-shirt, the perfect uniform for the invisible
woman. Avoiding eye contact, she hurried to her locker and
repacked her book bag, keeping her observation notebook
handy. She shut her locker and moved down the hall.

Steroid Boy came strolling up. He was all by himself. Gracie couldn't remember ever seeing him alone. And he was smiling … at *her*.

No way! she thought. It can't be Steroid Boy.

But he kept coming toward her, staring right at her.

When he was a foot away, she asked, "What?" The word came out meaner than she'd meant it.

"Excuse me?" Bryce, aka Steroid Boy, returned.

"What do you want?" Gracie asked, panic twisting in her stomach.

"My locker?" He nodded at the space behind her. "You're blocking it."

Gracie gasped and sprang from the locker as if it were on fire. "Sorry." She had to get a grip on herself.

Annie Lind and Michael Slater, a really cute sophomore, strolled up the hall together. Apparently, it hadn't taken Annie long to get over Nate. Gracie tried to take notes on Bouncy Perky Girl, but she couldn't think of a blog name for Michael. She tried to focus on his body language when he talked to Annie. But it didn't work. Nothing came to her.

Gracie moved farther down the hall and almost bumped into Julianne Gustaf.

"Be careful!" Julianne snapped.

*Be careful?* Gracie tried to remember the exact words Blog Buster had used. She didn't think they were "Be careful" exactly, but there had been a warning. And now this — this was a warning. Julianne worked on the school paper. What if she'd found *That's What You Think!* by accident? She probably spent a lot of time on the Internet. She might have been investigating —

But that was crazy. Julianne had already moved off down the hall, without a backward glance at Gracie.

Now, everywhere she looked, Gracie thought she caught people staring at her. She was the observed, not the observer. And she didn't like it one bit.

# 8

Gracie was actually relieved when the bell rang for first-hour classes.

Art was a lecture on Mondays. Gracie took a back-row seat and got out her art notebook. Jazz slid into the seat next to her. Gracie nodded, and Jasmine Fletcher returned the nod. She had her notebook out too and was doodling in the margins. Some of the doodles were caricatures of classmates. Others were animals. And they all looked amazing.

In front of them and off to the side, two freshmen seemed to be having an intense conversation. Their smiles stayed in place, and their voices were friendly. But their stiff shoulders and backs gave them away. It was a civilized fight. Gracie wouldn't have been surprised if one of the girls jumped up and bolted from the room. Normally, Gracie would have jotted all kinds of notes and observations. But this morning, she just didn't care.

Ms. Biederman started lecturing about lines and space. But Gracie couldn't focus. Instead of taking notes, she let her gaze wander to Jazz's notebook. In one margin, Jazz had drawn a big computer and a small computer. The monitor on the big one was blank, but colors swirled on the small screen. A word balloon had the big computer saying, "You're supposed to be in sleep mode, Junior." And the Junior computer answered, "I can't sleep. I was watching that Y-2K scary movie." Jazz had crossed out Junior's answer and tried another one: "I can't sleep. I don't feel so good. I think I've got a virus."

Gracie laughed.

"What?" Jazz frowned over at her.

"I ... I just ... Your computers. Your pictures?"

"What about them?" Jazz sounded so defensive.

Gracie wished she'd stayed invisible. But it was too late now. "They're good. Funny." Her voice cracked. She wanted to tell Jazz what she really thought. Not just about these drawings, but about the painting Jazz had torn up in class and about how talented she thought Jazz was. "I think you should draw more of your own stuff. You know? Your own way?"

Jazz tore out the notebook page and folded it in two. "Well, that's what *you* think."

Stunned, Gracie couldn't believe what she'd just heard. *That's What You Think!* Jazz had said it as if embarrassed at Gracie's compliment, as if the words didn't mean a thing.

But they did. Of course they did.

"What do you mean?" Gracie demanded.

"Doing things my own way gets me into nothing but trouble." Jazz made a face like she'd bitten into a rotten banana. "Why are you all up in my business, anyway? You're always taking those notes of yours. What's *that* about?"

The bell rang, and Jazz didn't wait for an answer.

Gracie stayed in her seat until the room emptied. It was crazy. Jasmine Fletcher was Blog Buster? It didn't fit with anything she'd observed about Jazz. She had Jazz pegged as the type who didn't care what other people did. She didn't seem to want other people in *her* business, and she seemed to do everything she could to stay out of theirs.

But here it was. The signs were all there — the computers, even the name of the site — *that's what you think*.

The rest of the morning, Gracie piled up evidence against Jasmine Fletcher. There was plenty of it too. And the most convincing piece was the fact that Jazz was Ty's big sister. Mick must have let something slip while she and Ty were playing ball. Either that, or Mick had decided she had to tell her best friend everything. Either way, Ty must have run straight to his sister and told her about the blog.

As the pieces clicked into place, Gracie got angrier and angrier — at Jazz, and at Mick. Mick had no business telling Ty. She'd promised to keep Gracie's secret. Now she'd broken that promise and ruined everything.

Every time she saw Jazz talking to somebody, Gracie figured she was telling them about the blog. Pretty soon everybody would know. Then what? It was like waiting for a hurricane to hit. She didn't know whether to board up the windows or get out of town fast.

As soon as school was over, she raced to her locker. All she wanted was to get out of there. She slammed the locker shut and started out. Halfway to the door, she saw Jazz coming toward her. All of Gracie's emotions balled together and morphed into pure anger. This wasn't fair. It wasn't right.

Without even thinking, Gracie stepped directly in front of Jazz, blocking her path in the packed and noisy hall.

"What are you doing?" Jazz asked.

"What are *you* doing, Jasmine?" Gracie returned.

"Get out of my way, Grace. You're blocking the hall."

"Am I? That's what *you* think." *I can be cryptic too*, Gracie thought. She knew she should stop there. She'd never done anything like this before.

"Excuse me?" Jazz was good. She had a look of honest surprise about her.

Kids flowed around them like they were boulders in a river. Gracie didn't care. They all probably knew anyway, thanks to Jazz.

"I know that you know," Gracie said. *"That's What You Think!* — my blog, my website. I know you know I'm Jane. And I know you're Blog Buster. So you can stop pretending."

"You know what? You need professional help, girl," Jazz said.

"Why are you doing this?" Gracie heard her own voice as if it came from someone else, someone desperate. This wasn't how she wanted to come off. She didn't want to sound needy. "Look. You'd never understand what this live journal means to me. I'm asking you to back off."

Jazz took a step back. "And I'm *telling* you to back off." She waited, hands on hips, until Gracie stepped aside.

Gracie watched her walk away. The whole horrible scene had been a disaster. She felt like she was going to hurl.

Gracie tore outside and started running as soon as she hit King Street. She kept on running. Her head pounded with every footstep. She'd pictured the encounter with Blog Buster in a hundred ways. And none of those imagined scenes had gone half as bad as the real thing.

This was why she kept her distance from people. She didn't know how to handle flesh-and-blood humans. That's why the Internet journal had worked for her. And why real relationships would never work for her. That's why everybody was better off when Grace Doe stayed invisible.

If only Mick could have kept her secret ...

Mick! She was the one Gracie should have gone off on — not Jazz. If Gracie had taken more time to think through things, she would have realized this, and the whole last hour could have been erased. It wasn't really Jasmine Fletcher's fault. It wasn't even Ty's fault for telling his sister. Gracie hadn't sworn *him* to secrecy.

Mick was the one who had promised to keep Gracie's secret. And Mick was the one who had broken her promise.

Gracie walked the last block home. Back at school, Luke would have waited for her for fifteen minutes, then left. Those were Luke's rules. She couldn't remember if Mick was riding home or walking. She glanced behind her, but didn't see Luke's car or Mick on foot.

Gracie tried to pull herself together before she opened the front door. Inside, the Doe house felt unusually quiet. She smelled brownies baking, and something else, something Italian and spicy. "Mick!" Gracie shouted.

"Shhh!" Lisa came trotting down the stairs, a laundry basket under one arm, Daniel under the other. "Hi, Gracie. Daniel refused to take his nap again. Are you hungry? I got groceries this morning. Grapes and peaches and yogurt."

"No thanks," Gracie said. "Is Mick home yet?"

"Nope," Lisa answered, hoisting Daniel higher on her hip. "I think she said she was going to 'create ice cream' after school. So I guess she's helping out at Sam's. Wish she liked to help out that much in *my* kitchen."

"Thanks," Gracie said, heading back out.

"Muh-eeeeeeee!" Daniel screamed.

Gracie ran back and kissed her brother before racing out once more.

She backtracked to King, then turned onto Main Street, speed-walking all the way to Sam's Sammich Shop. The shop was owned and operated by Samantha Lind, Annie's mother. It was the major after-school hangout for Big Lake's high school students. In Gracie's opinion, the sandwich shop felt more like an ice-cream parlor. They advertised twenty-five flavors of ice cream, and Mick was constantly trying to come up with Number 26.

By the time she got there, Gracie had worked herself up all over again. She burst into the crowded shop, ready to drag Mick outside and let her have it. Mick would have to make things right, no matter what it took. Somehow, she had to make "Jane" anonymous again.

Beach Boys music blared from the jukebox. Mrs. Lind had decorated the shop in retro 1960s style, a cross between funky beach and cool sixties rock. Black booths lined one wall, and a half dozen tables were scattered over the wooden floor. Old black-and-white posters of the Beatles hung above the booths. And in the back, one whole wall was a mural, painted to look like the beach, complete with an ocean and teens in swimsuits dancing in the sand. Mick joked that this ocean was the closest thing Big Lake had to a big lake. Mick, of course, loved the place. But Annie complained that her mom should spring for an update, something ill and twenty-first-century.

Gracie glanced around the shop for any sign of Mick. It threw her off balance to see so many kids going on as if nothing had happened in *their* universe. They were laughing, eating fries, and having a great time, while her whole world was caving in on top of her. Everything she'd worked so hard to create the last few months was collapsing. And all because Mick couldn't keep her big mouth shut.

Annie and her mother stood behind the counter, taking orders. Next to the long food counter was the ice-cream case, with twenty-five barrels of ice cream. Annie and her mom could have passed for sisters instead of mother and daughter. Same big blue eyes and perfect white teeth. Same size, probably about five feet ten. They both had auburn hair, although Annie wore hers shaped and straight, shoulder-length, and her mom's hair curled around her face.

Gracie took one of the three empty seats at the counter. Mick had said Mrs. Lind bought the stools from an old diner. They were silver chrome, the kind with no backs.

"Hey, Grace!" Annie's mother called.

"Hi, Mrs. Lind," Gracie said.

"I still want you to call me Sam, honey." She walked to Gracie's end of the counter. Annie was scribbling someone's order on a little pad. "So, can I get you something?" Sam asked.

"No, thanks," Gracie answered. "I'm just looking for Mick. Is she here?"

"She's helping in the back. It's been wild this afternoon. Your sister is still trying to come up with a new flavor, you know? She should be out in a minute." Sam waved to a policeman who was just coming in. "Tony!" she shouted. "I'll be right with you. The usual?" She turned to Gracie. "Gotta go."

A second later Annie came over. "Hi, Grace. Did you want anything?"

Gracie shook her head. Then she had a thought. "Annie, how well do you know Jasmine Fletcher?"

"She's a freshman, right? Killer hair. We're both on the homecoming committee. She's got the best ideas for decorations! Why?"

Gracie shrugged. "I just wondered. I don't know much about her." She couldn't ever remember talking like this with Annie. Yet Annie was smiling and chatting as if they were old friends. In all of Gracie's observations of "Bouncy Perky Girl," she'd never noticed this genuine interest of Annie's. Right now, in spite of all the others in the shop, Annie was focused on *her*, as if Gracie were the only person here.

"Jasmine painted the mural a couple of years ago." Annie pointed to the wall with the beach painting. "Pretty tight, huh? She doesn't like us to tell customers she did it though."

Gracie had always assumed they'd paid a professional to paint the mural. That's how good it was. "She did that in middle school?" But Gracie wasn't that surprised. Jazz had become her mortal enemy, but Gracie couldn't deny an amazing talent.

Annie's mother came back. "Are you talking about Jasmine? I'll bet it's been a year since she's been by the shop. How's she doing?"

Gracie shrugged. "I don't know her very well."

"They're a wonderful family," Sam said. Gracie noted the way Sam's mouth tightened. Something was not right, and it had to do with Jazz.

"Well," Sam continued, "you girls should go out of your way to be nice to Jasmine, if you can. They've been through a lot. I hope they're happy now."

"Are you kidding?" Annie asked. "They live in a mansion. Aren't her parents lawyers or stockbrokers or something?"

"Things aren't always that easy," Sam said.

Annie may not have caught the wrinkled forehead, the twitch at the corner of her mother's mouth, but Gracie did. "What is it, Sam?" she asked.

Sam rolled her lips over her teeth, a gesture that told Gracie she was wrestling with something. "I don't suppose it's a secret," she said at last. "But I wouldn't want you repeating it, just the same. It was years ago, and I don't think any of them ever got over it. Before the Fletchers moved to Big Lake, when they were still living in Cleveland, Jasmine's big brother was murdered."

# 9

"Murdered?" Annie repeated the word in a whisper. "For real?"

Her mother looked like she wished she hadn't said anything. "He was killed in a drive-by shooting. They never talk about it, as far as I know. But I can't help thinking it's never far from their thoughts."

Now Gracie felt even worse. She'd had no idea Jazz had gone through something like that. She couldn't even imagine losing Luke that way. No wonder Jazz was such a loner.

"That's awful!" Annie exclaimed. Her eyes filled instantly with tears. Her compassion was the real thing too. Gracie could see it. One more thing she'd missed seeing in Bouncy Perky Girl.

"Jasmine had an older brother," Annie continued. "I just didn't know. And then they've had all the problems with Kendra too. Can you imagine?"

Kendra was Jazz's sister. Gracie figured she must be about thirteen, a year older than Ty, a year younger than Jazz. But Kendra seemed much younger. She had Down syndrome and went to a special school north of town.

"I love Kendra," Annie said, swiping her cloth over the counter. "She's such a sweetie. Some of us cheerleaders performed at halftime and helped out at the Special Olympics last year. Kendra played on the volleyball team. She was so cute!"

Strike three on Gracie's observations of Bouncy Perky Girl. Gracie never imagined Annie, or any of the cheerleaders, would volunteer to help at Special Olympics. When she'd walked into the shop earlier, Gracie didn't think she could feel any lower. But she'd been wrong about that too.

She felt like she should say something to Annie or to her mother. But she didn't know anything to say.

Annie and Sam went back to waiting on customers while Gracie waited for Mick to come out of the kitchen. Finally, Mick emerged, carrying a tray of glass bowls with a scoop of ice cream in each. Suddenly, all of Gracie's mixed-up emotions came back together in a wad of anger. It was all she could do not to charge Mick right there. "Mick!" she shouted. "I have to talk to you."

"Hey, Gracie!" Mick called. "In a minute. Sam! You have to try this one — licorice peppermint." She set down the tray and waited for Annie and her mom to taste her creation.

Sam made a face, then tried to cover it with a grin. "Closer, Mick. Keep trying."

"What's in this one?" Annie asked, taking a spoonful of the second dish. At least the color was better in that one — yellowish instead of gray.

"It's apple-lemon," Mick answered, taking another spoon and tasting it herself. "Yuck. It's horrible."

"No argument here," Annie said, puckering her lips.

"Mick, I need to talk to you." Gracie tried to whisper, but it came out too loud.

"Give me a minute." Mick took the bowls containing the weird ice cream off her tray, leaving four dishes of chocolate. "I'll deliver these and be right back."

Gracie thought she'd spin off her seat waiting for Mick. Finally, Mick plopped on the stool next to her.

Gracie took a deep breath and leaned forward, so only Mick could hear. "Mick, how could you break your promise? I trusted you."

Mick looked as if somebody had slapped her. "What? What are you talking about?"

*"Blog Buster?* It's Jasmine Fletcher."

"You're kidding! Ty's sister? Are you sure?"

"Right in my face she said, 'That's what you think!' And she drew this thing with computers. I'm sure."

"But how — ?"

"You told Ty, didn't you?"

Mick shook her head. "No! I didn't tell him anything, Gracie! How could you think I told him, when you made me promise not to?"

"You tell Ty everything."

"Not this."

"It had to be you." Gracie felt like she was exploding inside. "How else would Jasmine know? Maybe you didn't mean to, but you did. And now it's all ruined. She knows, and she'll tell everybody."

"You've gotta believe me, Gracie. I didn't say anything to Ty or to anybody." Mick bit her upper lip and blinked.

Gracie spun the stool and turned her back on Mick. Her head throbbed and her chest burned. She heard Mick get up and run back to the kitchen. In all the years they'd been under the same roof, Gracie couldn't remember a real fight with Mick. They'd had a couple of spats over whose turn it was in the bathroom or who got the front seat. But never anything like this. And now it felt like things would never be the same again.

Gracie heard a familiar, obnoxious laugh. Storm Novelo blew in the door, as noisy and stormy as ever. She was wearing what she'd worn to school — a long, flowered dress, a fake flower in her hair, and flowered sandals. At least half a dozen silver earrings climbed her ears like stair steps. At lunch, Gracie had overheard Storm telling the cheerleaders that she was descended from a royal family of Mayans, which made her a Mayan princess. "Officially, I'm Mestisa," Storm had announced. "Part Mayan and part Spanish. I descend from a long line of Mayan princesses."

Gracie didn't know whether to believe her or not. Mostly, not. To avoid Storm, Gracie twirled back toward the counter.

"Annie!" Storm yelled from the doorway. "Wait 'til you see this!" She waved a fistful of papers.

"You made it!" Annie cried, running from behind the counter. "Come and meet my mom." They sat a couple of stools down from Gracie, who felt trapped.

Annie introduced Storm to her mother. They hit it off right away, which was no surprise. Everybody hit it off with Samantha Lind. And everybody hit it off with Storm.

"Hey, Grace!" Storm called. "Not working today?"

Gracie shook her head, amazed that Storm even knew who she was.

Sam brought Annie and Storm ice-cream cones, then headed toward the booths to help out the college girl who worked part-time.

As soon as Sam left, Storm slapped a pile of papers down on the counter. Gracie couldn't see too well from where she sat, but the papers looked like pages copied off the Internet.

Storm whispered something and pointed to a page.

"No way!" Annie said.

"Way," Storm insisted. "Read this one."

Gracie tried not to pay any attention, but she couldn't turn off the observer in her. She strained to hear what they were saying. Out of the corner of her eye she spotted Mick standing back behind the ice-cream machine, staring at the pages Storm was showing Annie.

"See? Tell me that's not Bryce!" Storm challenged. "And that's your science teacher, right? And that's definitely the principal."

Every nerve ending in Gracie's body went on alert.

"It's Big Lake High all the way," Storm said. "I knew it the minute I walked into that school. Okay. Maybe not the minute. But I knew it after the first day. Biederman's in there. And that English teacher."

"Seriously," Annie reasoned. "Maybe everybody who reads this stuff sees themselves in it. Like there are types out there or something."

Gracie knew better than to even hope Storm would go for that explanation.

"That's what I thought too, at first," Storm said. "But there are too many coincidences. Annie ... you're in here."

"I am not!" Annie shouted. She glanced around, then lowered her voice. "You're making it up."

Storm shuffled pages until she found the one she wanted. "Read this, you Bouncy Perky Girl, you."

Gracie felt sick.

"Bouncy what?" Annie took the page and read.

Gracie would have given just about anything to become invisible — really invisible. She tried to remember everything she'd written about Annie. Gracie stole looks at Storm. Storm's body language indicated that she was intrigued, but not angry. She was, in fact, loving this.

Gracie had written worse things about Storm. At least she thought Storm would think they were worse, especially the part about seeing through her happy act. But she hadn't posted that blog until late. Apparently, Storm hadn't read the latest blog entry. Either that, or she didn't recognize herself. Writers were always saying that people never recognized themselves in stories. Maybe Annie wouldn't recognize herself either.

Annie covered her mouth with her hands. "I can't believe this! This is *me!*" Annie stared, wide-eyed, as she read.

So much for that nonrecognition theory, Gracie thought.

"This really did happen to me!" Annie exclaimed, pointing at the page. "I was just trying to show everybody a new cheer. And he came up and yelled at me." She slammed down the page. "*I'm* Bouncy Perky Girl!" Annie sounded horrified. "Storm, have you shown this to anybody else?"

"Not yet."

"Well, don't! I don't want our whole school to start calling me the BP Girl! What if other kids are reading this too? Are they? Do you think they are?"

"Easy, girl. I doubt it," Storm said. "I read blogs all the time. I found this one about a month or so ago. It's really good, so I kept reading it. Then when I walked into Big Lake High, it was whack! I mean, I knew this was Typical High.

It was exactly like the school I'd been reading about. But seriously, what are the odds that somebody else at Big Lake would stumble onto the site? There are thousands of them on the Net."

Annie, her elbows on the counter, sighed deeply and thumbed through the printouts again. "Who's writing this awful stuff, anyhow? Jane who? I don't know a single Jane at Big Lake."

"Well, the name's a fake, of course," Storm answered. "I don't know who the real 'Jane' is yet. But I'm going to find out."

Gracie gripped the counter so hard her fingernail broke.

"Good. And I'll help! Come on!" Annie grabbed the papers, and Storm followed her toward a back booth. "I'll bet it's Ashley. Or Brittany. Or maybe Denisha. Unless it's a guy — like Eric, or Sean, or Dylan." Annie had made eleven guesses by the time they were out of hearing range. And not one guess was Gracie.

Gracie felt like she'd swallowed an anchor. She didn't know if she could move from the counter stool. How could she have gotten everything so wrong? *Storm* was Blog Buster. Not Jasmine Fletcher! She'd accused Jazz, faced her off in the school hall. Screamed at her.

And *Mick*.

Gracie turned toward the ice-cream counter. "Mick?"

But Mick was gone.

# 10

Gracie walked home the long way, crossing Brookside Park, then winding back through the run-down neighborhoods south of Main. She weaved through backyards in the Old West End, where the big houses hid behind monster maple trees. Someone had been burning leaves already, and the autumn smell filled her lungs.

She rehearsed what she'd say to Mick. Mick was more than a stepsister. Mick was her best friend, maybe her only friend. She'd helped set up the blog for no reason, except that she was Mick.

She tried Mick's cell. Voicemail picked up instantly. Mick could never remember to turn on her cell after school. Gracie hung up. She couldn't put what she had to say in a ten-second voicemail message.

How could she have thought that little Mick, "Mick the Munch," had betrayed her? And even when she did think it, why did she have to say it? Mick was the last person in the world she'd wanted to hurt.

Apologies didn't come easy to Grace Doe. She usually tried to do an end run around them. Sometimes she'd do something nice that let the other person know she was sorry. But this

time, she knew she owed a full-fledged apology. And she
couldn't rest until she'd given it.

Thunder rumbled, and Gracie looked up to see fast-moving
gray clouds. The air had changed, picked up speed, and stirred
up the smell of dampness and storm. Gracie walked faster. It
would serve her right if she got caught in a thunderstorm.

As soon as she thought it, a giant drop of rain splatted
on her arm. Another landed on her head. The sidewalk was
alive with dark spots that closed in on one another. Thunder
groaned again, and the sky ripped open.

Gracie ran the rest of the way. By the time she got home,
she was soaked to the bone. She came in through the garage
and kicked off her soggy shoes. David and Daniel were
banging on something in the kitchen, so she sloshed in there
to find Lisa.

Lisa was standing on a chair to reach a cookbook from the
top shelf. She took one look at Gracie and hopped down. "What
happened? You're soaked, Gracie! You should have called me.
The boys and I would have come and picked you up."

Gracie stared down at the puddle of water forming at her
feet. "I'm dripping. I'm sorry."

Lisa waved it off. "Don't worry about the floor." She
pointed toward the twins. "They've been decorating this floor
with Cheerios all afternoon. It's you I'm worried about. You
better get out of those wet clothes and into a nice, hot bath."

"I'm okay, Lisa. Thanks. Is Mick here?"

"Mick? She's at Sarah's. Remember? The big birthday
overnight."

Gracie vaguely remembered Mick's plans. Gracie couldn't
stand the thought of not talking to Mick until tomorrow.
"You're letting her sleep over on a school night?"

Lisa shrugged, palms up. "Dumb, huh? But Mick promised they'd have lights-out by nine. And you know Mick. She'll turn off those lights herself at nine if they're still on."

Gracie did know Mick, and Lisa was right. Mick kept her promises.

Gracie needed to talk to Mick, but she didn't want to call her when all her friends were around either. As much as she hated the idea, she was going to have to wait until tomorrow.

That night, for the first time since she'd started the blog, Gracie went to bed without writing a new journal entry. She just didn't have it in her.

The next morning, Luke and Gracie rode to school in virtual silence. Gracie tried Mick's cell twice. When voicemail picked up the second time, she threw her phone back into her pack.

A block away from school, Luke frowned over at her. "Gracie, you all right?"

Gracie shrugged. She hadn't been less "all right" since the day her mom packed up and moved out of the house.

"Anything I can do?" Luke asked. He glanced over at her, and Gracie read his face — the lowered eyebrows, the turn of his mouth. He was concerned, worried. About her.

Gracie forced a grin. She knew she was better at fooling people than they were at fooling her. "Thanks for the offer, big brother. Not necessary."

Instead of making observations in the school halls, Gracie went straight to art class and slunk to the back row. She didn't want to run the risk of seeing Annie and Storm in the halls. Still, she knew she couldn't go on avoiding them forever.

The room started filling up. Then Jazz walked in. Without slowing down, she moved to the back and sat two seats over from Gracie. Gracie watched out of the corner of her eye as Jazz pulled her notebook from her pack and began sketching.

Gracie wrestled with herself. She'd whacked out yesterday, accusing Jazz of being Blog Buster. She should just come straight out and apologize right now.

Gracie took a long breath, let it out slowly, then leaned over the empty chair toward Jazz. "Hey, Jasmine. About yesterday? I guess I kind of made a fool of myself."

"Uh-huh," Jazz agreed. She didn't look up from her notebook.

"I'm sorry I went off on you like that. I know now I was wrong about you ... and the website deal."

Jazz looked up at her. "Yeah. You were something else, all right."

She sure wasn't making this any easier. Gracie made herself go on. "You must have thought I'd gone over the edge or something. It's just that my website — "

"I didn't know anything about your website," Jazz said.

"I know," Gracie continued. "And I'm — "

"But I do now, thanks to you," Jazz interrupted.

"You do now?" Gracie repeated. "Wha — how?"

"You gave me everything but the IP number — most of it in high-density volume, as I recall. All I had to do was type in 'Jane,' 'school,' and 'That's What You Think.' Took a few tries, but I got it."

"You ... you got it? Got what?"

"Your blog, Jane. Not bad. You could use graphics though. Or pictures. It's kind of 'Plain Jane' as is — the look of it, I mean. Otherwise, you got stuff tight."

Gracie tried to get control. "Jasmine, I didn't mean for you to — "

"Greetings, fellow prisoners!" Storm swirled down the aisle and landed in the seat between Gracie and Jazz. "Don't mind me."

Gracie was pretty sure the stare Storm was giving her was filled with hidden meaning. She wanted to look away. Instead, she stared right back at her.

"You're wide-eyed as ever, aren't you?" Storm observed, locking gazes with Gracie. "Jasmine," she said, without turning away from Gracie, "did you know that ostriches' eyes are bigger than their brains?"

Gracie knew she had big eyes. At least that's what Mick and Lisa were always telling her. So this was some kind of crack about her brain. But she could not let Storm get to her.

Thankfully, Ms. Biederman shouted, "Get out your notebooks, class." And the moment passed.

It took Ms. B a few minutes to get people to settle down. "This week we're going to start using acrylics," she announced, as if granting her students the keys to the kingdom. "I want you to use them wisely. They cost an arm and a leg."

"What's that mean, anyway?" Jazz muttered, too low for Ms. B to hear.

"It's so cool!" Storm answered, loud enough so Jazz and Gracie could hear, but nobody else. "In the Victorian era, painters charged a set fee to paint the torso, like a portrait shot — just the head and shoulders. So if the guy being painted decided he wanted it to be a full shot, like with arms and legs, that cost extra. Get it? It cost 'an arm and a leg'!"

Jazz grinned, but the grin faded fast. "I meant, what does it mean to use acrylics wisely."

"Ah," Storm said, turning around and slumping in her chair. "No idea."

The rest of the hour, nobody in the back row took notes. But Gracie noticed two things, both about Storm: (1) She saw a flash of sadness cross Storm's face. It reminded her of what she'd seen at the grocery store. (2) She saw anger. And the anger was directed at Gracie.

Gracie told herself that she was imagining the anger. What had she done to New Girl, anyway? Why would Storm even notice her? But there it was, the strained neck muscles when she looked Gracie's way, the quick eye movements.

When class ended, Gracie tried to be the first one out.

Storm eased in front of her, blocking her exit. Then she leaned in and whispered, so low Gracie could barely hear the words:

"See you ... Jane."

# 11

The room spun. Voices faded into one another. Gracie stared at Storm, the words still pounding in her ear: *See you ... Jane.*

Storm knew. Somehow, she'd put it all together.

Annie Lind burst into the art room. "There you are! I thought you had art. Listen, Storm, I think I know who wrote the you-know-what!"

Storm turned away from Gracie to face Annie. "Yeah?"

"It's got to be Andrew or Rachel ... or Haley," Annie said, looking at her list.

Nate had followed Annie in. "Come on, Annie! You don't even return my phone calls now?"

Annie glanced at him and said sweetly, "Sorry, Nate. No can do." She pulled her cell out of her pocket. "I took you off speed dial."

"You *what*?" Nate sounded like Annie had taken him off oxygen.

"Finally," Storm commented. "That's legal proof of breakup, Nate. Time to give it up, guy."

Annie and Storm walked out together. Gracie stood in the doorway, vaguely aware of students filing out and other students filing in.

She was late to second-hour science, but Ms. Doyle, her teacher, either didn't notice or didn't care. Gracie opened her book and pretended to follow along, but the words floated around her, not making it to her brain.

More than anything, Gracie wanted to talk to Mick. She needed Mick's perspective on everything. Storm scared her. She wouldn't put it past her to announce the blog over the intercom or hand out business cards with *That's What You Think!* and the web address on them. Gracie thought about her website. She could have Mick take the whole thing down and maybe put it up later, with a different IP address. But she'd lose all of her loyal readers. And she barely had enough money for maintenance. She'd never get the start-up cash again. She had no idea what to do, and she'd never felt more alone.

She didn't see Annie or Storm again until lunch. Then she heard Storm's obnoxious laugh before spotting her at Annie's table, surrounded by a pack of guys. When the table burst into laughter after something Storm said, Gracie felt they had to be talking about her.

On the other side of the cafeteria, Jazz ate at a table full of jocks. Was *she* telling them about the website too?

Gracie dumped her lunch in the trash and wished for this day to be over.

Storm was in rare form in history class. Since Storm sat front-row, center-of-attention, Gracie took a seat in the back. But it wasn't far enough away. Storm entertained students *and* teacher — everyone, except Gracie. Annie laughed so hard, she had to keep wiping her eyes. But to Gracie, every joke, every comment, sounded like a threat.

During Mr. Stovall's dry lecture on inventions, Storm kept interrupting with her own list of "greatest inventions." Bones let her get away with it. Apparently, he enjoyed anything Storm had to say.

"What about Wite-Out?" Storm asked when the teacher was listing great inventions that had changed the face of America. "I mean, we don't need it much now — true enough — thanks to spellcheck and my personal best friend, the Delete key. But when it was invented ... Did you know the mother of Mike Nesmith invented Wite-Out? *The* Mike Nesmith, as in the leader of the Monkees? As in 'Hey, hey, we're the Monkees'? Anyway, it's so amazing what computers do now. Like people who use them for diaries." She turned around and smiled at Gracie, who quickly stared down at her desk.

Gracie knew Storm was going to tell the whole class about her blog. She just wanted to torture Gracie with it first.

A few minutes later, when "Bones," Mr. Stovall, talked about how misunderstood most inventors were, how society considered them crazy, Storm was at it again. "Writers are even weirder and more misunderstood than inventors though, don't you think? I heard Goethe could write only if he had an apple rotting in his desk drawer. And Mark Twain made them put tin on the roof of his expensive home so he could hear the rain."

Storm turned around and stared directly at Gracie. "You're a writer, aren't you, Ja — I mean, Grace? Do you have any weird habits? Like, what do you do for material?"

Half a dozen kids turned around and looked at Gracie as if they'd never seen her before and wondered what she was doing in their classroom. Gracie knew they had no idea she was a writer. They hadn't even known she was a student.

Gracie sank deeper into her chair and didn't respond to Storm's question. After a minute, Bones started up again.

Gracie didn't know how much more of this she could take. She focused on the big clock hanging above Bones' head. The hands seemed to be stuck.

Gracie had no idea what Bones had been saying when Storm burst into another tirade: "Don't you hate fakes?" she began, slamming her notebook on the desk arm of her chair. "Like how fast-food places will spray sugar on potatoes so it turns brown and looks like golden fries? I just hate it when something claims to be something it's not! Or when *somebody* claims to be somebody they're not! Take Panama hats, for example. Know where they come from? Ecuador!" Her voice got louder and louder, as if inciting the crowd to riot. "And don't even get me started on Betty Crocker! Again, no such person — hello? The Gold Medal flour people made her up when they started getting baking and recipe questions about their cookbooks and cake mixes.

"And another thing. Who's John Doe, anyway?"

Gracie's stomach lunged, as if trying to leave her body. She could not live like this. It felt as if a hundred-pound anvil were dangling over her head, and Storm was holding the rope.

After class, Gracie ran after Storm and caught up with her at the end of the hall. "We need to talk," she said.

Storm didn't slow down. "Hmm. Let me see. Do I need to talk with Jane? The answer is so 'no.'"

"Are you going to keep calling me Jane?" Gracie demanded.

"Sorry. Feel free to call me Blog Buster if it makes you feel any better."

Gracie planted herself in front of Storm as they reached the doorway. "Why are you doing this? Why do you care so much about my blog?" Gracie demanded. "What's it to you?"

Storm pulled Gracie to the wall, where they were out of the stampede of students trying to leave the building. "What's your blog to me? Nothing! Not one thing. And until today, it was just funny."

"Funny? It's not funny, Storm!"

"No. You're right about that. Now it's personal. I read what you wrote about me." She glared at Gracie.

"So?" Gracie snapped back.

"So," Storm continued, "you don't know what you're talking about! And you sure don't know me." She turned to walk away.

"I know what I see," Gracie muttered.

Storm wheeled around to face her. "Hey! I am what I am!"

Gracie couldn't be sure, but for an instant she thought she saw it again — the "other Storm," the "real Storm." And *that* Storm looked like she could cry and never stop.

"No, Storm," Gracie said quietly. "You're *not* what you are. You told everybody you're in our history class because you got kicked out of the other class. I'll bet you tested out of freshman history. Right? And English?"

She didn't answer.

"All those facts?" Gracie continued. "You *know* stuff. You don't pick it up on MTV. You're smart, and you don't want anybody to know. Now that's what I call stupid."

"It's none of your business!" Storm shouted.

"Just like my blog is none of *your* business," Gracie countered.

They stared each other down. Gracie remembered doing stare-downs with kids when she was in elementary school.

She usually won. Only this time it felt like nobody was
winning. Grace hadn't wanted things to come out this way.
She'd wanted to talk to Storm, to ask her about the sadness.
Only not like this.

"Storm!" Annie came jogging up and wedged herself
between them. She shoved her notebook in Storm's face. "I've
figured it out." She glanced at Gracie and smiled.

For a second, Gracie was sure Annie had finally guessed
right, that she knew Grace Doe was the author of the blog.
Somehow, even though it meant twice as big a threat of
exposure, Gracie felt a sense of relief, or maybe pride.

Annie tapped her notebook with her pen. "It's absolutely
either Kaitlyn, Lauren, Brianna, Jason, Jose, or Kyle. They're
the best writers in the whole school. It has to be one of them.
Who else could have done it?"

"Me." The word was out of Gracie's mouth before she had a
chance to stop it.

# 12

Annie turned and squinted at Gracie, as if Gracie had suddenly grown a third eye in the middle of her forehead. "Excuse me?" Annie said.

"Me." Gracie couldn't stop herself now. Something inside her had come untied. "Sorry to disappoint you. *I'm* the one who wrote the blogs. Me. Invisible Grace. You wouldn't have guessed that in another thousand guesses, would you, Annie?"

"I . . . I . . ." For once, Bouncy Perky Girl had lost her bounce.

"Don't feel so bad, Annie," Gracie said. "Nobody would have guessed. I'm invisible. At least I was until Storm showed up. I could walk right through you and your cheerleading buddies, and you wouldn't even notice. So how could you have guessed I was the one writing about our school?"

Annie's expression changed. "Not just our school!" Her eyebrows lowered, and her lips formed a straight, hard line. "You made fun of *me*. You made me sound like, like — "

"Like someone who would never notice someone like me?" Gracie's voice cracked. Her throat burned. If she didn't get out of there right this minute, she'd burst into tears. She could not let that happen.

Gracie ran out of school and raced across the parking lot. She took backstreets, not slowing down, even when the ground turned rough. She stumbled but made herself run even faster, welcoming the physical pain of her lungs gasping for air. Sweat trickled down her shirt. She fell crossing Elm Street but made herself get up and keep going. She wanted to be home. She wanted to talk to Mick. Mick would help.

Then she remembered. Mick wouldn't help. Mick probably hated her — just like Annie and Storm and Jazz and everybody else hated her. Why couldn't she go back to being invisible? Why couldn't everybody just leave her alone?

Except she was alone.

And for the first time in her life, Gracie didn't like it. *I don't want to need anybody. People leave.* She thought of her mom and fought off the longing to see her, to talk to her. Her dad hadn't left her, but they didn't talk either, not really.

Maybe that wasn't all Dad's fault. Gracie couldn't remember the last time she'd tried to tell him about her life. Her blog, her website, had become so important to her. Yet she went out of her way to hide it from him. Is that what she wanted? To be cut off like this? Maybe it was time to tell Dad everything.

At her front door, Gracie paused long enough to catch her breath and brush the dirt off her pants. *Please, let Mick be here.* The thought became a prayer. And she prayed it again. *Please, let Mick be here. I need her.*

For as long as she could remember, Grace Doe had told herself that she didn't need anybody. It hadn't bothered her to be on her own. But it bothered her now.

Gracie flung open the door and shouted, "Anybody home?"

"Gracie, come in here, please," Gracie's dad called from the living room. Gracie couldn't remember the last time he'd been home before she was.

"Dad? Is everything okay?" She felt dizzy as she walked into the room. Dad and Lisa were sitting on the couch, the TV off. "Is it Mick?" Her heart pounded. "Did something happen to her?" If something had happened to Mick, Gracie would never forgive herself.

"No, Gracie," Lisa said quietly, her voice soothing, as if she could read Gracie's mind. "Mick's fine. She called from Ty's and said she'd be home late."

Gracie felt such a wave of relief that for a minute, nothing else mattered. Mick was all right. *Thank you, God.*

"Gracie, we need to talk to you," Dad said, his voice cold, distant.

"Do you think I could call Mick at Ty's first? I want to — "

"This can't wait. Come in and sit down." Dad motioned for her to take the chair closest to the couch.

Gracie knew she was in trouble. She tried to imagine what else could have gone wrong. Was there anything left to collapse?

"We have a question to ask you, Gracie," Dad began. "Who is Jane?"

Gracie froze. She looked at Lisa instead of Dad. Lisa's eyes were soft, pleading. "I — I was going to tell you."

"A letter came this morning," Lisa explained. "It was addressed to Jane Doe. Since nobody here is Jane, I opened it, thinking maybe they got the name wrong."

"And it turns out," Dad continued, but not in the soft-spoken tone Lisa was using, "it's a bill!" He held out the bill to Gracie.

She took it. It was the same one she'd gotten in an email, plus another month in advance. Her web provider must not have gotten the check in time.

"Would you like to explain why we got a bill for someone named Jane at this address?" Dad demanded.

"Well, you shouldn't have," Gracie began. This was not how she wanted to introduce them to the blog. She wanted them to see that she could finance and run it herself. She wanted to share with them how important blogging had become, how it was helping her to be a better, more disciplined writer. She didn't want them to end up with the bill. "I paid it. Honest. We can tear this one up and — "

"So you're Jane now?" Dad asked.

Gracie could tell how hard he was trying to keep his temper. "No. Jane is just my ... my Internet name."

"Your Internet name?" Dad looked like he was losing it. "Tell me this isn't one of those cyber-dating things? One of those websites where people lurk and wait for young girls?"

Gracie kept shaking her head no. "It's not, Dad! I wouldn't be that stupid. I know what goes on over the Internet. This is *my* website. *I* control what's posted there. Nobody knows who Jane is. I blog — that's short for web log, like a journal. And I really did pay the bill."

"I don't think your dad's as worried about the bill as he is what the bill's for," Lisa said. She glanced from Gracie to Dad and back again. "Why do you owe these people money? What do you put on your site, honey? Why were you keeping it so secret? Why do you call yourself Jane?"

Gracie had tried so hard to keep her blog a secret. Now she wanted to tell them about it, and she couldn't find the words. It was almost funny. When she wrote, the words came. But now, in front of her own parents ... *Lord, please give me the words*. The prayer had just come, without her even thinking

about it first. She'd wanted Mick to be here, to help her say
what she needed to say. But now it was totally up to God.
*Please, make them understand.*

"Jane says what I can't," she began. "She writes about people.
She connects, *I* connect, with readers." And just like that, it all
came out. Her words filled the living room, spilling over and
bumping into one another as she cried. She told them about the
blog, the live journals. She told them about Blog Buster, about
accusing Jasmine, about accusing Mick. She talked about
Annie and Storm and how she saw things about them no one
else saw, but how, at the same time, she missed seeing so much.

To their credit, neither parent interrupted. Dad started to
twice, but Lisa's hand on his arm stopped him. As torn up as
Gracie was, she appreciated that.

When there was nothing left to say, Lisa got up off the
couch and sat on the arm of Gracie's chair. Then she leaned
over and hugged her. Gracie didn't hug her back, but she didn't
pull away. She felt Lisa's tiny arms around her shoulders.
Those arms were strong and gentle at the same time.

"Don't keep things like this inside, Gracie," Lisa said. "You
don't have to, you know."

"I'm not sure I understand," Dad admitted. "You wanted to
keep your website secret. Yet you want strangers to read it?
But now these other girls know it's you?" He tugged his right
earlobe, a gesture Gracie had observed for years. It usually
signaled pure frustration. "Maybe it's for the best. Can't you
go back to writing in a regular diary like you used to? The
one with the little gold key? Isn't that safer than these *snogs*, or
live journals, or whatever you call them?"

"It's not the same thing, Barry," Lisa said, joining him on
the couch again. "Gracie is a writer. Can you imagine the

discipline it's taken to come up with a column every day for two months?" She turned her smile on Gracie. "I have trouble writing the grocery list once a week."

Gracie knew Lisa was exaggerating. Before the twins were born, Lisa had run her own ad agency. It was how she and Gracie's dad had met. But she felt a rush of gratitude for Lisa.

"A writer?" Dad repeated. "You never told me you wanted to write. So you want to be a writer ...?"

Gracie thought she heard a note of pride in the question. She nodded. She *had* told him, of course. More than once.

Dad scratched his chin. "I always wanted to be a writer."

"You *are* a writer, Dad," Gracie said. Most nights he was home, her dad could be found in his den at his computer, working on an ad campaign, coming up with slogans and ad copy.

"I mean, I wanted to write a novel — not just ad copy."

Lisa stood up. "Well, buddy, you've still got a few good years left in you. It's never too late for the great American novel."

Dad stood up to follow her as she headed toward the kitchen. Then he turned to Gracie. "Are you going to keep that journal thing going on the Internet?"

Gracie thought about it. Was she? It had caused her so much trouble. But she couldn't imagine not having it. "I think so. I'd like to. I think."

"Are we going to be allowed to read it?" he asked.

"Anybody can read it," she answered, "but I'd rather not think of you two as regulars on my blog."

Dad sighed. "That's what I thought. Are you sure you have that bill covered? I don't want you working so much at the supermarket. School comes first, Gracie."

He was back to his usual self. "School comes first" was his motto.

"I know, Dad," she answered. "And the bill's taken care of. But ... thanks."

Dad followed Lisa to the kitchen, leaving Gracie alone in the living room. She felt drained. She wanted to replay what had just happened. She and Lisa and Dad had worked through something big, something more than her blog. She couldn't have said exactly what had changed, but she didn't feel so much like the odd man out.

*You did this, didn't you, Lord?* She could almost sense God smiling. *Thanks. Thanks for helping me say what I needed to say and hear what I needed to hear. And thanks for Dad and Lisa, for my whole family.*

*Mick!* She still needed to talk to Mick. But the phone seemed like a cheesy way out.

Gracie closed her eyes to think. Even when she was just thinking, it felt like God was listening. She pictured Mick. Gracie could still see the pain on Mick's face when she'd accused her sister of telling Ty about the website. Then Annie's face popped into Gracie's head. "Bouncy Perky Girl." There was a lot more to Annie than Gracie had imagined. Had Gracie hurt her too? Again, the image in Gracie's mind shifted and she could see Jazz. Jasmine Fletcher acted like she was angry at the world half the time. But she'd kept quiet while Gracie had ripped into her, accusing her of being the Blog Buster.

Thoughts of the Blog Buster conjured up images of Storm. Gracie didn't know much about Storm Novelo. But from what she did know, she believed Storm might be the loneliest person at Big Lake High. Even lonelier than Gracie herself. Because nothing made you feel more alone than pretending to be part of a crowd.

Or pretending *not* to be?

What if Mick was right? What if God had actually created people to work together like parts of a body? What if so many people felt so lonely because God had created them to belong? To need one another? Gracie knew she needed God. And Jesus. That was a given.

But other people?

She opened her eyes. Inside her head she could still see them — Annie, Storm, Jazz, and Mick. And there she was too. All of them were like puzzle pieces looking for a puzzle.

Gracie grinned up at the ceiling. She could almost hear God laughing. It had taken a lot, but she got it. Unless God decided to place her on a planet *without* people, no matter what she thought she wanted, Grace Doe was not alone. She was part of the puzzle.

Gracie dashed up the stairs. She knew exactly what she had to do. She just didn't know if it would work. She was going to write. She knew what she needed to say. And this time, she was going to say it, no matter where it took her.

Gracie typed as fast as she could, knowing full well that this could be her last blog ever. And as she typed, she prayed that Mick, Storm, Annie, and Jazz would read it ... and care.

• • • • • • • • • • • • • • • • • • • • •
## THAT'S WHAT YOU THINK!
SUBJECT: I'M SORRY

*This is a different blog than I've written before. I apologize to my readers, but this one is for four people: Bouncy Perky Girl, New Girl, Jazz, and the Munch. I'm praying you'll read this, guys, and at least give me a chance to tell you I'm sorry. So here goes.*

*First, I'm sorry. I'm not very good at this apology thing. I spend so
much time by myself. I guess I'm pretty lousy when it comes to
people. But I mean this and hope you believe me. Munch, you're
the most loyal person I know. And I'm so sorry I didn't trust you. BP,
I was baggin' on you without knowing you. Then I bit your head off
for no reason. (Not that I'm saying there might not be a reason ever.)
Jazz, same goes for you. I knicked out, got all out of order. You didn't
deserve any of it. New Girl, I sized you up — all wrong — the first day.*

> *FLASH: This isn't working for me. Doing this on the
> Internet is whack. I don't want to be a ranker. I want a
> face-to-face. If you're reading this, will you give me a
> chance? Meet me at closing time, where ice cream is
> invented. Please?*

> *Jane*

Gracie knew it was the worst blog she'd ever written. The
hardest. And the most important.

Now she had to pray they'd read it ... and give her another
chance.

# 13

Gracie made herself play catch-up with homework the rest of the night. Twice she picked up the phone to call Mick, then hung up. She wondered if Mick had talked to Jazz while she was at Ty's. What if they didn't even read the blog before tonight? She should have given them twenty-four hours and asked to meet tomorrow instead of tonight. Or what if they read her blog and just didn't care enough, or were too angry, to come?

She left early for Sam's Sammich Shop. At least she was confident none of the girls would have trouble figuring out "where ice cream is invented." Closing time on weeknights was eight o'clock, and Gracie tried to time it so she'd arrive just before closing. She wanted to catch them all together and say what she had to say one time.

Gracie talked to God as she walked, grateful she wasn't going into this alone. By the time she turned up Main, the sun had set. Enough light remained to keep the streetlights from coming on. She walked slowly, making herself stop and stare into store windows to kill time. All the shops were closed. The cool breeze carried the scent of coffee from the Main Street Diner. A flock of geese honked, but she couldn't see their V shape in the dark sky.

When Gracie arrived at Sam's Sammich, Annie's mom was saying good-bye to the last two customers. She flipped the Open sign over to Closed.

"Grace! Are you looking for Mick?"

Gracie's heart sped up. "Is she here?"

"I haven't seen her, honey," Sam answered. "She didn't come by tonight."

"I — I kind of asked her to meet me here at closing," Gracie said. "I can wait outside though," she added quickly.

Sam jerked her head, motioning Gracie inside. "Don't be silly. Come on in."

"Thanks. I don't want to make you late." Gracie glanced around the empty shop. Tables were cleared. The main light had been dimmed. She was beginning to think it was a dumb idea to ask people to meet in a shop after it closed. "Is Annie here?" she asked, feeling awkward.

Sam shook her head. "No. I think she and Storm went to the library. I'm not sure."

"Really?" Gracie asked, trying not to give in to the urge to give up and go back home alone. "I — I sort of asked Jasmine to come by. I was hoping Annie and Storm would show up."

"Annie didn't say anything to me about it," Sam said. "But you're welcome to wait as long as you like." She moved behind the counter and clicked off a couple of lights in the back. Then she came out again. "You can lock up when you're finished, okay? You've watched Mick do it often enough." She tossed Gracie the big ring of keys.

Gracie caught it. "Thanks."

"I'd stay and wait with you, but I promised to stop by the nursing home and see Mrs. McGraw. You sure you're okay alone?"

Gracie had to smile. Being alone was the easy part. Being part of something with other people, that was what she'd always considered the hard part. "I'll be fine, Sam. Thanks for letting me wait inside."

Waiting was tough. Too much time to think. While she spun on one of the stools, Gracie replayed each fight she'd had that week, each fight *she'd* started. First with Jazz. Then with Mick. Then with Storm and Annie. She checked her watch. What made her think any of them would come and meet her now?

She was so lost in thought, she didn't see Mick until she heard a tap on the door's glass pane. There was Mick, her baseball cap turned backward, a glove in one hand, a bat in the other.

Gracie ran to the door and pulled it open. "Mick, I'm sorry. I'm so sorry!" She hugged her sister and wondered when she'd hugged Mick last.

"It's okay, Gracie." Mick's voice was muffled, since Gracie had her in a bear hug. "You were freaking out. I understand. Your blog's important to you."

Gracie pulled away from Mick, but held her by the shoulders. "Yeah. But you're more important than a thousand blogs. I can't believe I said those things to you, or thought you'd — " She stopped. Behind Mick was another figure, much taller.

Jasmine Fletcher brushed by them and into the shop. "Touching, but I still have homework to do tonight."

Gracie, stunned, let go of Mick and followed Jazz inside. "Jazz, thanks for coming."

Jazz turned and raised one eyebrow at Gracie.

"I mean 'Jasmine.' Sorry about that."

Jazz shrugged. "Jazz works." She plopped onto a stool and stretched out her long legs.

"There's a lot I want to say," Gracie began. "But mostly, I'm really sorry. I had no right to scream at you like that in the hall."

"It *was* pretty whack. But worth it. Your website's tight. I never would have found it on my own." Jazz glanced around the shop. "So, where *is* everybody?"

Gracie stared around the room too, as if she expected to see Annie and Storm hiding in one of the booths. Pale light shone from the kitchen. The dimmed overhead bulb turned the rest of the shop hazy, taking the edges off chairs and booths, counters and stools. Gracie could imagine the shop looking like this in one of her dreams. "You guys are the only ones who came."

"Annie didn't show?" Mick asked.

The door burst open. As if on cue, in came Annie, followed by Storm. "I'm bouncy and perky and bouncy!" Annie shouted, skipping past Gracie to the counter and taking the middle stool.

"Annie!" Mick cried. "I knew you'd come."

"So where's the famous ice cream?" Storm asked, taking the stool between Annie and Jazz.

Gracie couldn't stop staring at them. "I can't believe it. You guys came?"

"No," Annie answered. "*We're* invisible. So maybe you're seeing things."

So they'd come. But as Gracie observed them, she knew this was far from over. Storm's forehead was wrinkled. Jazz kept her hands in her pockets and refused to look into anyone's face. Annie's "perk" was fake, and her foot tapped furiously against the counter.

They were here, but they were angry.

# 14

"Look," Gracie began. "I'm sorry I got in your face, Annie."
She walked over and stared down at Bouncy Perky Girl.
"I just — no, I'm not going to make excuses. I'm lousy with
people. That's pretty obvious. It's not your fault that you're
popular, and I'm not — not that I'd ever *want* that. Anyway, I
shouldn't have taken stuff out on you."

Annie twisted in her stool. "No, you shouldn't have." She
took in a deep breath, then let it out. "But you were kind of
right, Grace, about that invisible stuff." She looked up at
Gracie and smiled. "I'm sorry too."

Gracie hadn't expected that. She didn't know what to say.
As hard as it was to make an apology, it felt even harder to
accept one.

"The thing is," Annie continued, "I just get so caught up in
my own life that I don't see anybody else."

"Unless it's a guy," Storm added.

Gracie studied Storm. She'd be the hardest one to apologize
to. But she had to try. "Storm, I'm sorry I went off on you.
And if I made you feel bad by writing those things, I — "

"Enough," Storm interrupted. "First Amendment. Freedom
of speech. Yada yada yada. So, is that it?"

"Yeah," Jazz said, acting like she was ready to bolt. "So, is my work here done?"

"No!" Gracie motioned for Jazz to sit back down. "Please?"

Jazz sank back down onto the stool.

Gracie studied the four faces staring back at her. An idea had sparked when she'd started writing the message to ask them to meet her here. Since then, all she'd thought about was getting the chance to tell them how sorry she was. Now she'd had the chance, and she'd taken advantage of it. But the idea that had been just a whisper was growing into something more like a shout.

Mick broke the silence. "Gracie? What's up?"

"It's the blog," she began.

"Well," Annie said, her stool swirling side to side, "we won't rat you out, if that's what you're worried about. Right, Storm?"

Storm popped her gum. "Yeah. Blog Buster is retiring."

"So," Annie went on, "you can go back to the way things were, right?"

That was true. Gracie could go back to the way things were. She could do everything by herself.

Or could she?

"Look," Gracie said, "I have an idea." She turned to Mick. "Mick, will you still help me with *That's What You Think!?*"

"Of course."

"So you're all set then," Annie said. "Keep up the good work!"

"But I can't," Gracie said. "Not unless you'll help me."

"Me?" Annie asked. "I'm not much of a writer. Your columns are spun! I've learned all kinds of things reading your blogs, Grace. Like, I never knew you could read people and tell what they're thinking, if they're lying or nervous, like that. You don't need me, girl!"

"Annie, I've got a mailbox full of comments and questions from kids about dating and boy-girl relationships."

"Yeah. I saw a couple of those comments on your site," Annie said.

"I can't answer those questions," Gracie admitted. "I'm fine with questions about other relationships — teachers, parents, friends even. But guys? No way! You could have your own love advice column, Annie. Right on the site. Like a 'Dear Annie' column."

"Cool!" Storm exclaimed. "Or a 'Dear BP' column."

Annie elbowed her. "Wait a minute. Are you saying you want *me* to write something on *your* blog, Grace?"

Part of Gracie wanted to back out, to say no — she was just kidding. She could handle the blog on her own. But the pieces were coming together. And the puzzle was bigger than Grace Doe. "I want you to help. I need you, Annie."

Mick came over and gave Gracie's arm a squeeze.

"Cool." Annie seemed to be considering the possibilities. "This could be so fly! Seriously. There's a whole world of girls out there who don't have a clue when it comes to guys. And vice versa. I suppose I owe it to them to share my expertise."

"Talk about being overqualified for the job," Jazz observed.

Storm swiveled to give Jazz a high five.

Annie frowned up at Gracie. "Do you really think I can do this?"

Gracie nodded.

"Maybe you could be 'Professor Love'!" Storm suggested.

But Gracie wasn't finished. "Listen, Storm. I know we haven't exactly gotten off on the right foot."

"Really?" Storm asked. "I hadn't noticed."

"Okay. I deserve that," Gracie admitted. "But you could have a weird-fact column on the blog. A 'Did-You-Know' section, where you pour out all those facts ... you know, the ones you pick up on MTV?" She grinned.

Storm returned the grin. She didn't answer, but Gracie could tell she was at least thinking about it. "Hmm. Might be better than letting the facts seep out in classes."

"Exactly!" Annie agreed.

Ideas were coming at Gracie so fast, she didn't have time to sort them out. But they were coming together. "Jazz, you already saw why I need you."

"Graphics." She and Jazz said it at the same time.

"You could doodle," Gracie suggested. "Or you could come up with a cartoon whenever you felt like it! That would be so cool, Jazz!"

Jazz turned her napkin around. She'd drawn a picture of half a dozen flies walking with picket signs. One sign read: "We want a better name!" The next picket sign said: "*Fly?* Are cockroaches named *Crawl*?" A cockroach in the corner carried a sign that read "So what's in a name?"

"Yes!" Gracie shouted, laughing. "See? You *have* to join this blog team, Jazz!"

"Wow!" Annie exclaimed. "So we're all part of the *That's What You Think!* blog? This is spooky. It's just like that verse you put up on the website."

Gracie didn't get it. "What verse? I didn't put up any verse."

"Yeah you did," Jazz insisted. "Something about the whole body working together and everybody having different gifts. Like some are toes or something?"

Gracie turned to Mick.

Mick never could hide anything. "I might have slipped in that verse after I read your blog tonight. Thought it might help."

Gracie would have gone crazy if Mick had done anything like that before. But not now. The blog had become bigger than Jane. It didn't even feel like it belonged to Gracie anymore. "So maybe you'll be doing more than maintaining the site, huh, Mick?"

"Yeah," Storm agreed. "Like feeding us ice cream, for example?"

"Great idea!" Annie said. "Let's seal the deal with ice cream!"

"I know just the flavor too," Mick said, scurrying behind the counter and disappearing into the kitchen. "Go sit at a table, and I'll be right there."

They moved to the nearest round wooden table and pulled up another chair, making room for the five of them. While they waited for Mick, they laughed and joked. And Gracie felt part of all of it. She wasn't invisible, not now. She couldn't have gathered together more different girls if she'd tried. Yet here they were, in an ice-cream parlor, in the near-dark, as if they'd always been friends.

"You're crazy though," Storm said, pointing at Gracie. "You do know that."

Gracie stopped laughing. Something inside her started to harden.

Storm turned to Annie. "And you? You're definitely postal."
She turned toward Jazz. "Hey. Anybody who paints voices has
to be psycho, right?" Her gaze traveled from one of them to the
other. "Don't worry about it. All of my friends are crazy."

Gracie relaxed. This was how friends teased each other.
"What a coincidence that all of your friends are crazy," she
observed. "I'm guessing it's the primary qualification for the
position, Storm."

Storm looked surprised, then pleased. "Touché, fearless
leader."

They laughed harder. Then they talked about the blog.
They decided to keep the name *That's What You Think!* And
they'd all have their own section of the blog. Annie would
write her love column. Storm would have a trivia fact section.
Jazz would create a cartoon and add graphics. And Gracie
would keep blogging, writing her live journal, based on her
observations of human nature.

By the time Mick came back with her tray full of ice cream,
they had the blog all worked out.

"Ta da!" Mick cried. "My special creation."

Gracie groaned. She'd tried dozens of Mick's ice-cream
disasters. "Give it a rest, will you, Mick? Don't you have any
chocolate back there? Or even vanilla?"

"I have faith in you, Mick," Storm said. "After all, Frank
Epperson invented the Popsicle in 1905, when he was only
eleven."

"Where do you get this stuff?" Jazz asked, taking a bowl
and a spoon from the tray.

Mick set the other bowls around the table. Then she took a
seat too.

"What flavor is it, Mick?" Annie asked, sniffing her bowl of mud-colored ice cream.

"It's kind of a surprise," Mick said.

Gracie felt like gagging, and she hadn't even smelled the creation yet.

"What about M&M's on top?" Annie suggested, as if stalling the moment of truth.

"Great idea!" Mick agreed. She sprang up and ran to the kitchen. When she returned, she carried a cupful of candies, which she sprinkled on top of each dip of ice cream.

"You know, don't you," Storm began, "that M&M's are battlefield candy."

Jazz groaned.

Storm continued, as if uninterrupted. "Soldiers ate them in the Spanish Civil War because they didn't melt in their pockets. Mr. Mars, of the future Mars Bars, saw the candies and took it from there."

"Well, I like the yellow ones best," Jazz said, picking a yellow candy off Storm's ice cream.

"They all taste the same," Storm explained. "Identical ingredients."

Mick passed out spoons. "Ready?"

They exchanged anxious looks, dug in their spoons, and took their first bite at the same time, as if they were entering the Synchronized Eating Olympics.

"Mmm," Jazz murmured.

"Man, it's spun, Mick!" Storm exclaimed.

"You did it!" Annie shouted, taking another bite.

"I can't believe it," Gracie said, amazed at how good the ice cream tasted. "You've got to tell us what's in it."

"Cranberry, lime, marshmallow, and peanut butter!" Mick replied.

"Mick!" Gracie cried. "You hate all of those flavors."

"That's the idea," Mick explained. "It's my theory. If I put four different ingredients together, even ingredients I don't like much, something wonderful will happen when they're mixed together."

"*Five* ingredients," Annie corrected. "Don't forget the sprinkles on top."

Gracie wondered if the others were thinking what she was. *They* were five very different ingredients. Maybe together, they could be something good too, something better than they'd each been on their own.

"You know, Munch," Gracie said, taking another bite, "you're pretty amazing." Mick would be the M&M's in this creation. A little of Mick sprinkled on top could go a long way. "Yep. I definitely think you're onto something."

"I think we're all onto something," Annie added.

Storm got that teasing look in her eyes that Gracie was getting used to. "As they say," Storm pronounced, "that's what *you* think."

Gracie laughed. But it *was* what she thought. She looked at the girls sitting around the table, from Annie's cheerleading uniform, to Mick's baseball cap, to Jazz's wild hair, to Storm's dangling earrings, to her own black camouflage. Only God would have dreamed of bringing these pieces together. She could see that now, finally. And she couldn't wait to see where they'd go from here.

# Internet Safety by Michaela

People aren't always what they seem at first, like wolves in sheep's clothing. Chat rooms, blogs, and other places online can be fun ways to meet all kinds of people with all kinds of interests. But be aware and cautious. Here are some tips to help keep you safe while surfing the web, keeping a blog, chatting online, and writing emails.

- Never give out personal information such as your address, phone number, parents' work addresses or phone numbers, or the name and address of your school without your parents' or guardian's permission. It's okay to talk about your likes and dislikes, but keep private information just that—private.

- Before you agree to meet someone in person, first check with your parents or guardian to make sure it's okay. A safe way to meet for the first time is to bring a parent or guardian with you.

- You might be tempted to send a picture of yourself to new friends you've met online. Just in case your acquaintance is not who you think they are, check with your parent or guardian before you hit send.

- If you feel uncomfortable by angry, threatening, or other types of emails or posts addressed to you, tell your parent or guardian immediately.

- Before you promise to call a new friend on the telephone, talk to your parent or guardian first.

- Remember that just because you might read about something or someone online doesn't mean the information is true. Sometimes people say cruel or untruthful things just to be mean.

- If someone writes creepy posts, report him or her to the blog or website owner.

Following these tips will help keep you safe while you hang out online. If you're careful, you can learn a lot and meet tons of new people.

## Subject: Michaela Jenkins

Age: 13 on May 19, 7th grade at Big Lake Middle School
Hair/Eyes: Dark brown hair/Brown eyes
Height: 5'

"Mick the Munch" is content and rooted in her relationship with Christ. She lives with her step-sis, Grace Doe, in the blended family of Gracie's dad and Mick's mom. She's a tomboy, an avid Cleveland Indians fan, and the only girl on her school's baseball team. A computer whiz, Mick keeps *That's What You Think!* up and running. She also helps out at Sam's Sammich Shop and manages to show her friends what deep faith looks like.

## Subject: Grace Doe

Age: 15 on August 19, sophomore
Hair/Eyes: Blonde hair/Hazel eyes
Height: 5', 5"

Grace doesn't think she is cute at all. The word "average" was meant for her. She dresses in neutral colors and camouflage to blend in. Grace does not wear makeup. She prefers to observe life rather than participate in it. A bagger at a grocery store, only her close friends and family can get away with calling her "Gracie." She is part of a blended family and lives with Dad and step-mom, two step-siblings, and two half brothers. Her mother's job frequently keeps her out of town.

## Subject: Annie Lind

Age: 16 on October 1, sophomore
Hair/Eyes: Auburn hair/Blue eyes
Height: 5', 10"

Annie desperately wants guys to admire and like her. She is boy-crazy and thinks she always has to be in love. She considers herself to be an expert in matters of the heart. Annie takes being popular for granted because she has always been well-liked. She loves and admires her mom. Her dad was killed in a plane crash when Annie was two months old. Annie helps out at Sam's Sammich Shop, her mom's restaurant. She can be self-centered, though without being selfish.

## Subject: Jasmine Fletcher

Age: 15 on July 13, freshman
Hair/Eyes: Black hair/Brown eyes
Height: 5', 6"

Jasmine is an artist who feels that no one, especially her art teacher and parents, understands her art. She is African American, and has great fashion sense, without being trendy. Her parents are quite well-to-do, and they won't let Jasmine get a job. She has a younger brother and a sister who has Down syndrome. She also had a brother who was killed in a drive-by shooting in the old neighborhood when Jazz was one.

## Subject: Storm Novello

Age: 14 on September 1, freshman
Hair/Eyes: Brown hair/Dark brown eyes
Height: 5', 2"

Storm doesn't realize how pretty she is. She wishes she had blonde hair. She is Mayan/Mestisa, and claims to be a Mayan princess. Storm always needs to be the center of attention and doesn't let on how smart she is. She dresses in bright, flouncy clothing, and wears too much makeup. Storm is a completely different person around her parents. She changes into her clothes and puts her makeup on after leaving for school. Her parents are very loving, though they have little money.

# 1

Annie Lind read the latest question emailed to the *That's What You Think!* website. It was a love question, and Annie's job was to field all questions about love. No problem. Not for "Professor Love," as Annie had started calling herself.

Grace Doe, a sophomore like Annie, had rounded up staff for her blog, which she called *That's What You Think!* Grace did most of the writing, putting out live journals about things she observed at Big Lake High School. But she'd recruited Annie to answer all love email.

"So?" Grace's long fingers drummed the back of the chair as she read the screen over Annie's shoulder. "Don't just sit there. How are you going to answer it, Annie?"

"I'm thinking!" Annie snapped. Grace could be so bossy. She and Annie had never been friends at high school. They had nothing in common. Annie belonged to everything— cheerleading, committees, Student Council. Grace belonged to nothing. Annie hated being alone. She needed her group of girls around her—or better yet, a group of guys. Grace, of course, liked to be alone. When Annie thought about it, it was pretty amazing that she and Grace could work together on anything.

Grace was growing on her, though. The girl saw things nobody else did. She knew when a teacher was going to explode, just by the way the teacher's nose twitched. She could tell if a guy was lying by what he did with his hands. She could see through people. Annie admired that.

She smiled up at Grace to make up for snapping at her. "Just give me a sec, okay?"

Grace shoved her short blonde hair away from her face and sighed. She was cute, with big hazel eyes. But it was like she didn't want anybody to notice how cute she really was. Everything Grace wore was either black or camouflage. Annie, on the other hand, majored in cute. Or at least she tried to. She knew a lot of kids, especially guys, thought she was cute. But she felt too tall, and her feet were definitely too big.

Annie scrolled down to see the other questions from readers. She winked at Mick, Grace's little stepsis, who was sprawled on the gigantic leather couch. The three of them had come straight to "the Cottage" after school so Annie could use the main computer and Mick could upload it to the blog site.

Annie wished she lived in a cottage like this. She loved everything about it—the big wooden beams, the fireplace, the white stucco walls. The plush, all-white furniture wouldn't have lasted thirty seconds at Annie's house, with Marbles the Mutt. Grace was so lucky. The cottage sat empty most of the time because Grace's real mom was usually off in Paris or London or someplace exotic. But she kept the cottage in their little town of Big Lake, Ohio, so Grace could use it whenever she felt like it. Since Grace had recruited her "blog team," they'd started using the cottage as a base camp.

The team consisted of Grace and Mick; Jazz, the artist; Storm, the trivia queen; and Annie. Each of them had a section of the website, and the whole thing was anonymous. Jazz did graphics and came up with cartoons that rocked. Storm wrote the same way she talked, spilling out all kinds of funny facts about everything. Annie, as "Professor Love," was supposed to do an advice column. She liked being Professor Love, but she was so busy she couldn't waste much time with it today.

She finished reading the last question and got ready to answer. "No sweat, Grace. Prof Love is on the case!"

• • • • • • • • • • • • • • • • • • • •

## THAT'S WHAT YOU THINK!
By Jane
SEPTEMBER 12

*Dear Professor Love,*

*I am SO in love with this boy @ my school, but i can't get him 2 love me back. I've done everything. I know his work and practice schedules, so I go 2 all his football practices and shop @ his store until I'm flat broke. I know his class schedule, and I dress hot every day and wait 4 him outside his classroom. Sometimes i drive by his house, just so i can "feel" his presence and hope he'll feel mine. What else can I do 2 make him love me?*

*—Desperate*

*Dear Desperate,*

*So what is your plan here? Stalk him and hope he'll panic and give in? There are laws against you, you know. Did you ever hear of a time-tested strategy called "playing hard to get"? No? Didn't think so. Try it! Soon—before the police show up on your doorstep. There's a chance—a small* chance—that he'll miss your adoration and wonder why you no longer know he exists. True, he may just be glad to be rid of you. But even so, isn't it better to move on than to be locked up in juvie for stalking?

Love, Professor Love


Dear Professor Love,

My boyfriend is picky. My girlfriends say he's controlling. I'll show up for our date in a skirt, and he'll suggest I go back and change into jeans. Another night, I show up in jeans, and he asks why don't I wear that red dress he likes. I guess it's more than clothes. He's always telling me not to laugh so loud, or to wear my hair up, or he's telling me to learn more about art and music. I don't want to make him mad or anything. But do you have something I could tell him?

—Unsure


Dear Unsure,

Yeah. Tell the loser that you're not Burger King, and he can't have it his way.

Love, Professor Love


Dear Professor Love,

All year I've been trying to ask out this hot girl in my English class. She's all I can think about—perfect bod, perfect everything. Only thing is, I've noticed that she can be, well, mean to other people. We sit next to each other in class, and *she's always bagging on this heavy girl who sits in front of us. And she giggles when a kid in our class, a special needs guy, answers a question wrong. Plus, she's always gossiping about other girls we know.*

*So, any advice for me?*

*—Starstruck*

*Dear Starstruck,*

*Here's my advice: See no evil. Hear no evil. Date no evil.*

*Love, Professor Love*

"Sweet!" Grace exclaimed as soon as Annie quit typing. "I couldn't have come up with those answers in a million years."

Annie leaned back in the cushy desk chair and sighed. "Nothing to it, when you're Professor Love. I think I was born to be a professor of love."

Mick came over and read the screen. "Annie, have you always known what to say to boys?"

Annie thought about it. "Well, since the age of four, anyway."

"Great," Mick muttered. "Want me to upload it now?"

Michaela, or "Mick," was only in the seventh grade, three years behind Annie and Grace, but she was the computer genius who'd set up the blog and kept it going. She helped out at Sam's Sammich Shop, Annie's mom's place, all the time. Mick was like the little sister Annie never had. One night a week, Mick had dinner at Annie's house, and Annie knew her mom looked forward to it as much as Annie did. Girlfriends her own age had come and gone for Annie. Boyfriends, too. But Mick had always been there.

"All yours," Annie said, giving up the computer chair.

As usual, Mick's long brown ponytail was pulled back through the hole in her Cleveland Indians ball cap. One of these days, Annie planned to take Mick under her wing and teach her to dress like a girl. She was already fiercely cute. In a couple of years, Mick would be amazing, inside and out.

Mick took over at the keyboard and started her magic. "I was hoping to talk to you about something, Annie."

"Sure, Munch." Annie could never say no to Mick the Munch.

"Great! I'll be done with this in just a minute." Mick popped in her keychain drive and hit Save.

Somebody's cell went off. Annie and Grace grabbed for their bags. It was Grace's. She flipped up her cell lid. "Hello? Hey, Storm. Where are you? You owe me a trivia column."

There was a pause. Storm Novelo had moved to Big Lake the last week of August, just after school started. She was a year younger than Annie and Grace, a freshman. But Annie liked hanging out with her. She was so kickin' cool. Nobody dressed like Storm Novelo.

"Yeah," Grace was saying into the cell, "well, I've got to have it by Saturday."

Grace listened, her ear pressed to the cell. Her gaze shot to Annie. "She's here. Just a minute." Grace passed her cell to Annie. "Storm wants to talk to you."

Annie took the phone. "Hey, girl!"

"Hey yourself," Storm answered. "Thought you might be with Gracie. You better charge your cell. I couldn't get it to ring. Guess where I am?"

"Ummm . . . the mall?"

"Nope."

"School?"

"Guess again."

"Home?"

Grace broke in with her deep, loud voice. "Excuse me! You're on my cell minutes. Play guessing games on your own time."

"I heard," Storm said, before Annie could repeat the warning. "I'm at a little place called Sam's Sammich Shop."

"I should have told you I wasn't working today," Annie said. She didn't work there every day because of cheerleading practices and other stuff. Today, her grandparents were covering for her. "Maybe I'll come by later if—"

"Later?" Storm interrupted. "Something tells me you're going to get your first speeding ticket getting over here right now. Or you would, if you actually had your license."

"Why?"

"Because guess who's here, sitting at a booth on the other side of the room."

"Ummm . . ."

Grace glared at her. Annie wondered if she knew they were starting another guessing game.

"Just tell me!" Annie demanded.

"Sean."

"Get out! No way!" Annie cried.

"Way."

Annie chewed on a piece of her hair that had just gotten long enough to chew on. "When did he get there? Do you think he's looking for me?" Sean Davis was the hottest guy at Big Lake, and Annie was in love with him. Totally in love with him. Never mind that they hadn't actually gone out yet. She knew. She just knew. And she was sure he felt it too. It was like they were soul mates.

# faiThGirLz!™
### 2 corinthians 4:18
## Inner Beauty, Outward Faith

# «Blog On»

Discover a world where girls come together from completely different backgrounds and beliefs to start a journey of faith and self discovery.

The new Blog On! storyline in the Faithgirlz!™ series encourages girls to use internet technology to stay connected to life, each other, and God. Life in the internet age can be a minefield for kids; potentially dangerous, it also has the ability to unite and connect kids with their friends and families and in powerful new ways.

## Available now at your local bookstore!

### Love, Annie

Softcover • ISBN 0-310-71094-4

Annie Lind was born to be "Professor Love," her website column for the lovelorn. She knows how to handle guys! When her dream date asks her out, she thinks she's in love—and neglects her friends and commitments. It'll take some guidance from an unexpected source to teach her what real love is.

### Just Jazz

Softcover • ISBN 0-310-71095-2

Jazz is working on a masterpiece: herself... Jasmine "Jazz" Fletcher is an artist down to her toes; she sees beauty and art where others see nothing. And her work on the website is drawing rave reviews. But if she doesn't come up with a commercially successful masterpiece pretty soon, her parents may make her drop what they consider an expensive hobby to focus on a real job.

### Storm Rising

Softcover • ISBN 0-310-71096-0

Nobody knows the real Storm... not even Storm! The center of attention wherever she goes, Storm Novelo is impetuous, daring, loud—and a phony. Convinced that no one would like her inner brainiac, she hides her genius behind her public airhead.

## Available now at your local bookstore!

## Inner Beauty, Outward Faith

My Faithgirlz™ Journal
0-310-71190-8

Faithgirlz™ NIV Backpack Bible
Italian Duo-Tone™, Periwinkle
0-310-71012-X

No Boys Allowed:
Devotions for Girls
0-310-70718-8

Girlz Rock:
Devotions for You
0-310-70899-0

Chick Chat:
More Devotions for Girls
0-310-71143-6

## Available now at your local bookstore!

zonder**kidz**